Love & Hope

Holidays in Hallbrook

Elsie Davis

Sweet Romance Publishing

Sweet Romance Publishing

Sweetromancepublishing.com

PO Box 778

Liberty, NC 27298

*To Mom
Thanks for all the love and support
you've given to guide me through life,
and for helping me to believe in myself and my
dream of writing.
I'm thrilled you enjoy my sweet and always happily-ever-after stories
and appreciate all your efforts to make them
perfect!
Happy Mother's Day!*

Romans 12:12

*Be joyful in hope, patient in affliction, faithful in
prayer.*

Chapter One

♥

GRACE STOOD BACK TO look at the three outfits she'd picked out for her first day at her new job tomorrow. One of them had to be just right, but which one? When she'd interviewed with one of the partners for the administrative assistant position at World Sport Inc., she'd been as impressed with his approachable attitude and appearance as he'd been with her resume and overall marketing experience. He'd made it clear that as Mr. Walker's assistant, she would not only oversee the office, but also their marketing.

Essentially, during the startup of a company, people typically wore many hats. She'd be one of those people. Grace understood completely and had been thrilled when the man had practically hired her on the spot. And she'd accepted without a second's hesitation.

It was a stroke of luck that the new online sporting goods retailer was opening a warehouse in Lancaster and that Grace had come across the job posting. Not to mention, a welcome relief after months of searching for new employment and just in time for her to catch up on bills and a past-due mortgage payment.

Lancaster was a bit of a drive from Hallbrook, but something she'd done frequently when she visited her mom and sister. Twenty-five minutes tops, which was doable. Winter always had its own set of issues with the roads, but Grace would deal with that situation after she was established and had proven herself as an asset to the company. By then, she hoped to have a little wiggle room.

She'd moved to Hallbrook for the quiet life five years ago after she graduated college and never regretted it until she got laid off from work. It gave her the space she sometimes needed from her family, the pair of them a bit overwhelming at times. Now, she loved the town and didn't want to leave.

Not being able to work from home anymore was the biggest disappointment in losing her previous employment. The job itself hadn't been all that exciting. But then, how could you glamorize over-the-counter medication, like antacids and hemorrhoid cream. And then there was the flood of prescription drug commercials that required every disclaimer in the book for all the awful side effects as compared to what the drug was intended for. Her ads had been creative, even if borderline ridiculous at times. They were also mentally draining. The downsizing had been met with mixed emotions.

Lucky moseyed into the bedroom and jumped on the bed. "No, girl. Get off my clothes, please." Blue-gray dog hair wasn't the professional image she was striving for.

Grace moved the outfits out of the dog's way. It was easier than making Lucky get down, not to mention she rarely told Lucky no for anything. Her dog was not only her best friend, but she was her confidant, so it was a good thing she could only bark and not talk. Grace shook her head and grinned as Lucky laid her head down on the comforter, her big eyes and oversized gray floppy ears too cute for words.

Grace picked up the light-blue blouse and dark-navy skirt and held them up in front of herself, checking out her reflection in the mirror. The outfit was professional, but it didn't reflect much of her personality. "What do you think, girl?"

Lucky raised her head and almost immediately laid it back down.

"I agree. Not very noteworthy for a first-day appearance." She tossed them back to the bed and eyed the black pants and white blouse. Again, professional but not individual. First impressions were huge, and since she hadn't met the man who would be her new boss, she wanted to get the look just right. Jordan Tate had reassured her that his partner was a great guy and would be easy to work with, but that hadn't lessened her tension.

Grace looked at the last outfit she'd chosen as a possibility. She shed her clothes and pulled on the white knee-length pencil skirt and then slid the satiny taupe blouse over her head and tucked it in for a cleaner line. The outfit looked good but still needed something. She glanced in her closet, her gaze landing on a pair of taupe above-the-knee boots she'd splurged on a year ago and only worn once since.

Working from home had its limitations when it came to opportunities to get dressed up and go out on the town, especially in Hallbrook, New Hampshire—a place where country living, church, and old-fashioned traditions came together.

She slid the boots on before grabbing the pink long sweater wrap hanging in the closet. Grace stepped back and checked out her image in the mirror, liking what she saw. This was perfect. Professional and yet creative. Exactly what her new boss would expect from her.

"Does this meet with your approval?" she asked Lucky. The dog rolled over, bored with the conversation and wanting a belly rub. Grace couldn't resist, and she paused to sit next to her canine bestie. Three minutes was all she could give this time, no matter how much Lucky rolled around on her back, begging for more.

"All done, and back to work for me. You're the most spoiled dog I know." But she was also the sweetest dog Grace knew. She'd gotten Lucky from a rescue shelter for springer spaniels. It had turned out to be the best decision ever made. The dog was loyal, obedient, and a great companion. Exactly what she had needed a few years ago.

Grace hung the other outfits back up in the closet. Placing the one she'd picked on a hanger to keep it from wrinkling., she hung it up on the bathroom door, out of Lucky's reach. Grace moved to the dresser and opened her jewelry box, picking out a pair of earrings and laying them on the nightstand.

The doorbell rang, and Lucky raised her head, one ear cocked toward the door.

Woof. Dog speak for someone's at the door, in case Grace didn't already know. Lucky jumped off the bed, raced ahead of Grace, and planted herself at the front door. Early on, Lucky had appointed herself as guard dog over the house and owner.

Not expecting anyone, Grace peered through the peephole. Living alone, you could never be too careful. She was surprised to see her cousin standing there with her baby daughter, Holly, firmly planted on her hip.

She pulled the door open, happy to see them. "This is a nice surprise. Come on in and let me take this cutie pie from you." Grace reached for Holly. The little girl was happily holding out her arms, just as eager to see her favorite...and only aunt. Karen's rocker look hadn't lessened in the months since she'd become a mom. If anything, she'd ramped up the facial jewelry, leather clothing, and tie-dyed hair. It wasn't a look Grace could go for, but to each his own as far as she was concerned.

"Thanks. Sorry I didn't call first, but I wanted to surprise you." Karen smiled as Lucky nudged her leg, looking for attention. She quickly gave the dog a pat on the head and then retrieved the bags sitting on the front doorstep.

"You certainly managed that." Grace hugged Holly and kissed the top of her head, inhaling the sweet scent of baby shampoo and innocence. Holly had just turned a year old last month, and Grace had been at the party, completely smitten with her cherub face and bubbly personality.

Her cousin was one of those footloose free-spirited women who didn't plan much in life, letting life come to them. *Including Holly*. At nineteen, Karen hadn't accepted her new role as a mother. But then Karen's mother, Grace's aunt, made it easy for her to ignore those responsibilities. Aunt Helen watched Holly every day while Karen went off to do whatever it was that Karen liked to do all day. Which pretty much amounted to nothing, unless it had something to do with her rock band. She'd been out of school eleven months, and so far, she only had a part-time job to show for it. "Can you stay long?" Grace asked.

"*Ummm*, unfortunately, I really don't have time." Karen had moved into the living room and set her things down. That was when Grace noticed how many bags her cousin had brought in. A baby required a diaper bag when they went places, but this was a bit overboard.

"That's a shame. So, what brings you to my neck of the woods? This is quite a way from Concord for a surprise visit." Grace held Holly up in the air and pretended like she was flying, then lowered her down slowly and blew bubbles on her stomach. The little girl giggled every time Grace repeated the motion.

She glanced at Karen when she didn't answer right away.

Her cousin was staring back at her, looking un-comfortable. She looked down at the diaper bag and began fumbling with the zipper, neither opening nor closing it. "I have a favor to ask of you." Karen let out a heavy sigh. "I don't have anyone else to ask."

"You can ask me anything. Let me guess, you need a babysitter. You know I'd love to keep Holly. Just say the word." Grace relished any time she could spend with the baby when Karen dropped her off for a few hours.

"Well, it's something like that. I'm sure you've heard Mama broke her hip." Her cousin looked up at Grace.

"Oh, no, I hadn't heard. When did that happen? How is she?" Holly reached for a lock of Grace's hair and pulled, trying to get her attention. She covered the baby's tiny hand with her own to still the motion, not relishing the feeling of having her hair ripped out.

"It was last week. I was sure your mother would've called and told you. But here's the thing, she can't watch Holly anymore, and it could be a while before she's fully recovered and mobile enough to keep up with the baby, and I need a sitter."

Grace immediately saw where this was going. She moved to sit down in the armchair, setting Holly on her knees for a horsey ride, but far enough away the baby couldn't reach Grace's hair. For the past two months, while she'd been unemployed, she would've loved the opportunity to watch Holly. It just wasn't possible now. "I see. Unfortunately, I got a new job with World Sport Inc., the new online sporting goods retailer that opened a warehouse in Lancaster. I start tomorrow morning. There's no way I can help you out. I'm truly sorry. You know how much I love spending time with Holly."

Karen sat back on the sofa, her mouth in a childish pout, her arms folded across her chest. "I should've known better." She shook her head, visibly upset. "This isn't fair. One mistake. And I'm supposed to pay for it with the rest of my life."

"What do you mean? What's going on?" Grace knew Karen had been having a tough time, but this sounded more desperate and more self-absorbed. Not the direction she'd hoped her cousin would go as she adjusted to parenthood. It was time for Karen to step up—not step back.

"The baby. It's no secret. She was a mistake. The father's out of the picture and I'm the one who's stuck. I have an opportunity of a lifetime to travel with the band to California. We were offered a gig, and as the lead singer, the future of the band has been laid at my feet. I can't very well take a baby with me."

The age-old battle between youth and adulthood was at war in her cousin. By the sounds of it, her youth was still winning. "Holly's a sweet baby. Maybe you need to focus on her, and new doors will open for you."

The petulant look on Karen's face showed her immaturity. "I don't want a new door. I worked hard getting this one. Please, isn't there anything you can do to help me out? You're the only one I can trust to take good care of Holly. I'm not a horrible person. I just don't want to be tied down and miss out on my own dreams."

Grace didn't know what to say. The timing was terrible. "How long are you expecting to be gone?" She shouldn't even be considering it, but she was.

The temptation to have Holly around was calling upon the maternal instincts that had been in overdrive lately.

"Three weeks tops. You won't regret it, I promise. Holly loves you." Karen stood, hope in her eyes.

Other people managed full-time jobs and children all the time. Something Grace had tried to convince the adoption agency of, except they'd turned down her application anyway. Her dream of adopting ripped away. She was still dealing with the heartache of rejection. In a way, she could relate to how Karen felt about having to give up her dream. Sometimes, life wasn't fair.

It wasn't Grace's fault that as a teenager she'd had polycystic problems that left her unable to have her own children. And it didn't change her ability to provide love, support, a roof over a child's head, and extended family. Being single shouldn't have excluded her from the happiness she could bring to a child's life. Unfortunately, the agency disagreed.

She was single and would remain that way. It hadn't taken her long to figure out men reacted differently to the news of her infertility. One, they left. Two, they lied and said it was okay. Or to be fair, they might have changed their minds. Three, they stuck around longer because they never wanted marriage or a family. Either way, the first two groups left her, and the third, she dumped them.

Grace would have been okay remaining single if only her prayers were answered for a child of her own. Maybe God was giving her the opportunity to prove to the agency they were wrong about her.

It was crazy to even consider watching Holly, given the fact she started a new job in the morning. There was no way around it. She had to report to work. The answer, of course, was for the babysitter to find a babysitter. Easier said than done, but it was worth a shot. Tiny waves of excitement rippled through Grace as hope blossomed.

"I've got an idea. Let me make a phone call to Faith and see if she can watch Holly when I'm working. I'm not making any promises. Are you sure you want to be away from the baby that long?" Grace wanted to make sure Karen understood the implications of her choices. There were always consequences to every decision one made.

"Thank you for trying. And, yes, I have thought about it, more than you can possibly imagine. But this is my big chance to do something with my career, and I want to take it."

"Okay, then." Grace pulled out her phone and dialed her sister's number. "Hi, Faith."

"Hiya! What's up? I'm just on my way out the door to go to the movies with friends."

"Are you working anywhere yet?" Her mother had just about given up hope of Faith growing up and joining the real world of work and responsibility, but Grace had convinced her that at twenty, her sister was still young. There was plenty of time for tough love.

"Just part-time over at the Piggly Wiggly bagging groceries. Not exactly a dream job, but it pays for my movies and fun money, I guess. Mom is after me to get serious, and maybe I will after this summer. I just want to have fun for a while." It was the same tune Faith had been singing since she graduated two years ago. Her sister's youthful excitement reminded her of Karen.

There appeared to be a lot of that going around with young kids these days. Grace shook her head. Whatever happened to going to college and getting a good job or starting at the bottom and working your way up the ladder? Both were acceptable routes. But starting out your adult life satisfied with movie money wasn't exactly promising for the future.

Grace had to find a way to entice her sister into accepting her proposition. "What if I offer you a full-time job babysitting for the next few weeks? It would be temporary, but it would pay well. And then maybe you can find something steady."

"But you don't have a baby? Unless those stork stories I heard growing up were really true." Her sister laughed at her own joke, but Grace wasn't impressed with the deflection.

"Babies don't come from storks. I'm talking about Holly."

"Why would you be watching Holly? Oh, wait. I get it. Aunt Helen can't watch her because she broke her hip. So how is it that she's with you and you're trying to find a sitter?"

"Karen's here at the house, and she brought the baby. She needs help while she pursues a career opportunity. I want to help her, but I start a new job tomorrow. For me to help Karen, I need you to help me. It would be at my place from eight to six, Monday through Friday. Just think, you get to play with a baby all day and get paid." Grace was trying everything she could think of to make it sound appealing, wanting her sister to agree.

Keeping Grace for three weeks would soften the devastating blow the adoption agency had delivered. For Grace, coming home to a baby at night would be amazing, even if it was only temporary. Not to mention, it might help Karen work through her issues. Perhaps she'd miss Holly enough to want to come home and *stay* home with her daughter.

"I don't know. That's like full-time." Her sister was stalling, trying to find a way to say no. Grace couldn't let it happen.

"Come on, Faith. It'll be fun. Think of all the extra time you and I can spend together. You've always wanted big-sister time. Now I'm offering it." And maybe, just maybe, she'd help her sister grow up through this process as well as Karen.

There was nothing but silence on the other end of the line. "Fine. I'll be there in the morning." Grace let out a huge breath of relief. This was going to work, and she was going to be a bona fide mother for three weeks. Best news ever.

"Thanks. You won't regret this. Tell you what, meet me at the Sweeter Side of Life in the morning, and I'll even treat you to your favorite pastry and coffee. You can stay with me these next few weeks if you want." It would be fun. A sister and a baby. Grace was ready for more excitement.

"The bakery sounds good. Staying with you, not so much. You're worse than Mom when it comes to rules." It was true. But only because her mother was lax with Faith. Her sister had been a late-in-life baby, born almost eight years after Grace, and right at the time when their father had deserted them. As a result, her mother had spoiled Faith.

"Fine. Meet me at seven." Grace hung up the phone and turned back to Karen, who stood watching with a lopsided smile plastered on her face.

"The answer is yes? You'll do it?" her cousin asked, hope lacing her voice.

"Yes." Grace nodded. "Holly and I are going to play house for a few weeks. Aren't we, sweet girl?" Grace hugged the baby tightly, excitement racing through her body and love overflowing from her heart. It wasn't the smartest thing she'd ever agreed to, but it was one of the most heartfelt and loving things she could do. Not to mention...it just felt right. After all, it might be her one chance to take care of a baby like this. Even Lucky seemed to sense the joy, the dog licking Holly's arm to show her some love.

"Yay! I'm going to California!" Karen exclaimed, dancing in circles. She threw her arms around Grace and Holly, hugging them both. "Thank you. You won't regret it."

Lucky barked several times, joining in the excitement even if she didn't understand what was going on.

"I hope not. If I lose my job because I can't make it work, I'll be looking to you to pay my bills here, Miss Hot Shot Superstar." Grace shook her head and laughed, unable to believe what she'd just agreed to.

"We're just opening for a band, but it really is a good opportunity." Karen's smile was infectious when she spoke of her music.

"You have a beautiful voice, and you have a passion for music. Let your light shine, and it'll be good." If Karen was going to chase her dreams, she needed to do it with all her might, so that when she returned, she'd be ready to settle down to real life. And in real life, breaking into the music world with any flourish was next to impossible.

"Thank you. Let's just hope you're right. I was optimistic and brought you a few baby things. Some diapers and clothes and bottles." Karen pulled each thing out of the bag, showing her as she rattled off the items. It explained the extra luggage. One whole bag was filled with toys. "I've got a pack 'n play in the car and her car seat. I'll be right back with them. And then I have got to leave. The band really wants to hit the road tonight, it's a long drive across the country, and none of us could afford to fly."

"Cutting it close for me to say yes, weren't you?"

"Let's just say, based on the circumstances I was hoping you wouldn't say no."

"Circumstances?" Grace frowned, glancing up at her cousin.

"You know, like, the fact you can't have kids. I once heard my mom and your mom talking about it. I'm sorry."

"It is what it is. I'm glad you thought of me, and you're right, it would be hard for me to say no to Holly."

Karen left to get the pack 'n play, and Grace sat down in the armchair, Holly on her lap. This was insane, but she'd make it work. "We can do this, can't we, Holly?"

The little girl touched her face and smiled, her soft chubby fingers poking at Grace's mouth to investigate. Luckily, she hadn't bothered to put on any earrings today. The last time she'd held Holly, the pretty pink and white beads had been too much to resist, and the baby had practically ripped one out of her ear.

After Karen returned with the pack 'n play and car seat, it didn't take her more than ten minutes to clear out after saying her goodbyes to Holly. Grace wasn't sure how she had the strength to leave, but then she hadn't walked in Karen's shoes and wasn't willing to pass judgment.

Grace completely put the job out of mind, preferring to focus on her charge. Tomorrow would come soon enough, and she'd start in her new role as administrative assistant and marketing guru. Tonight, however, was all about Holly.

After setting up the portable crib in her bedroom, Grace put away the baby's things. Holly was intent on exploring, which made the task take twice as long as she tried to keep up with the baby. Lucky followed Holly around like a second mother, trying to get used to her.

Once Grace had everything put away, she set her sights on feeding the baby. That sounded easy but turned out to be anything but. It didn't take long for Holly's face to be coated in a yucky-smelling green mush from the jar of food Karen brought, some of which made it into the baby's hair, turning dinner into dinner and a bath.

Hoping bath time would be less complicated, Grace filled the tub with only a few inches of warm water, testing it frequently. Holly loved the water, her laughter and splashing a joy to watch. There wasn't much in the way of water toys, but the bright-blue loofah and headrest pillow kept the baby occupied. Next time, she'd remember to have more toys for the baby. Maybe then there'd be less water on the floor to clean up afterward.

Grace used only a dab of her body wash on the baby, and only a washcloth on what little hair the baby had, not wanting to risk getting soap in her eyes. She kept a tight hold on the baby's arm since her skin was silky soft and slippery.

Wrapping the baby in a towel, she carried her to the bedroom, and laid her on the bed to put on a fresh diaper and pajamas. Before long, the two of them settled down in front of the TV to watch a Mickey Mouse cartoon. With Lucky sleeping peacefully at her feet, and Holly snuggled in her arms, the moment was almost perfect. Her prayers had been answered, even if it was only temporary. She had a baby.

Chapter Two

♥

THE ALARM WENT OFF way sooner than Grace would've liked. Whether it was because of too much excitement or new surroundings or both, Holly hadn't fallen asleep right away, which meant Grace hadn't gotten much rest. It hadn't taken much crying from Holly for Grace to give in and let the baby cuddle next to her in bed.

Not long after that, the baby settled down and drifted into sweet slumber. Only then had Grace turned the lamp to low and closed her eyes. She wouldn't hesitate to make the same choice again, hating the idea of Holly being scared or lonely. Lucky, on the other hand, hadn't appreciated the plus-one in bed and had slept on the floor.

Grace silenced the alarm, glancing over at Holly who was still fast asleep. She rolled out of bed, careful not to wake the baby, but determined to take advantage of the free time. It was a good thing she'd showered yesterday, because it was out of the question this morning. If the baby had been in her pack 'n play, a shower would've been easier to pull off, but short of waking Holly to put her in it, there was nothing else that could be done. And there was no way she was leaving her unattended and free to crawl where she couldn't see her.

Something else Grace would need to figure out. Karen had mentioned a baby monitor, but a search had turned up nothing of that nature. It would be the first thing on her shopping list if she didn't locate it this morning. And next on the list was bath toys. None of the ones Karen had brought were even remotely suitable.

After dressing in the outfit she'd laid out yesterday, Grace brushed her shoulder length hair into place, thankful it was a simple cut that was more wash and wear than wash and style. Every few minutes, she checked on Holly, which only impeded her progress to get out the door on time.

She'd barely managed to get a dab of makeup on before she heard Holly stirring. Grace went into the bedroom and crossed the room to sit down on the bed beside the baby, hoping to reassure her as she woke up in a strange place.

"Good morning, sweetheart." Grace smiled, grabbing her tiny fingers and pulling them to her mouth for a kiss.

Lucky jumped on the bed. "Good morning to you, too." She rubbed the back of Lucky's head, scratching her favorite spot behind her ears. "Don't be so jealous. She's just a little baby, and you're still mommy's little girl."

The dog seemed satisfied and laid down, her head facing Holly so she could keep an eye on her.

Holly sat up and stuck her thumb in her mouth, gazing at Grace and then at the dog. The baby lunged toward the dog, awkwardly falling on her, causing Lucky to suddenly pull back and jump down. Holly tried to follow, and Grace caught her by the feet just in time to keep her from tumbling off the bed.

Something else she needed to remember. Babies didn't have a sense of distance when it came to drop-offs, and it was up to Grace to protect her.

Maybe it wasn't such a good idea to let the baby sleep on the bed.

Holly laughed and crawled into Grace's lap, hugging her. The baby felt ten pounds heavier with her diaper full to the point of exploding. Of course, the telltale signs of moisture leaking through to her pajamas was another indicator.

"Stay here for a minute while I get a new diaper and some clean clothes." Grace crossed the room to the dresser and got out what she needed, keeping an eye on Holly to make sure she didn't try to get down again. Call her overprotective, but Grace wasn't sure what to expect...her lack of experience showing.

After changing Holly, she picked her up, using her hip to support the baby and held her tight. She grabbed the diaper and tossed it in the trash, the wet mass landing with a thud. It would stink if she left it there very long.

Mental note to self—empty the trash when I get home.

Grace glanced at the bed, scrunching her nose in dismay. There was no time to make her bed this morning, something else to put on her to-do list for tonight. It was totally unlike her, but there was nothing she could do about it now. She glanced at her watch, realizing they needed to pick up the pace.

Once Holly was safely strapped in her highchair, Grace mixed up a small bowl of the powdered flake cereal, following the directions. Sitting next to the baby, she tried to spoon-feed her, but each time she got near with the spoon, Holly smacked at her hand, knocking the concoction onto the tray, some of it making it as far as the floor. Apparently, this wasn't a favorite.

There was no time to use the internet to search for ways to make it better and Grace gave up, knowing they were on limited time.

A pastry wasn't the best breakfast for the baby, but it wouldn't be the worst thing either. Grace fixed a bottle, the smell as she added water enough to gag her. How could a baby drink something that smelled so nasty? Between green mush and this, it was a wonder babies ate or drank anything.

Grace screwed the lid on tightly, grateful the odor became trapped inside. She handed the bottle to Holly, letting the baby sit on the floor to drink it.

Grace used the opportunity to feed and put out clean water for the dog. Turning her focus back to the diaper bag, she unloaded some of the food and formula to make room for an extra change of clothes and plenty of diapers.

Holly finished the bottle in no time at all, barely giving Grace time to drink her coffee. Lucky stayed on the other side of the room, watching them both, and ignoring her breakfast. The dog only bothered to pick up her head and check things out when the baby banged the bottle of milk on the tray. Grace would need to make sure she gave Lucky plenty of extra attention when she got home tonight, the dog's jealousy evident.

After rinsing her cup and putting it in the dishwasher, Grace rechecked the diaper bag's contents. Satisfied, she slung the bag over her shoulder, picked up the baby, and put her on one hip. With her other hand, she picked up the car seat.

She wished she'd thought to put the seat in the car last night. Advance planning didn't seem to be her forte when it came to baby care. It would take some getting used to, but she was sure she would get the hang of it. Grace just hoped it would be sooner rather than later.

"Be good, Lucky. Hold down the fort till mommy returns." The dog wagged her tail but didn't move to join Grace at the door like she normally would.

Grace drove through town, feeling blessed to find a parking spot not far from the Sweeter Side of Life. She was only ten minutes behind schedule, which, to her way of thinking wasn't bad for her first day of parenting. Glancing around the cozy bakery, she searched for Faith. Her sister hadn't arrived yet, and Grace moved to stand in the line at the counter. It wasn't unusual for her sister to be late, so flipping the panic button would be a bit premature. But by the time Grace reached the counter, ten minutes had passed, and Faith was still a no-show. There was no way her sister would stand her up, would she?

Grace moved up to the register to place her order, refusing to step aside and wait for her sister to arrive. With her luck, a long line would form if she did, and then she'd really be late for her first day on the job. Faith would just have to take what she got when it came to pastries—the price of being late.

"Good morning, Grace. Who's the little cutie pie?" Amanda, the owner of the bakery, reached across the counter to rub Holly's arm. It always fascinated Grace how people loved to touch babies, wanting to share in the cute joy and happiness.

Grace smiled. "Morning. This is my cousin's little girl, Holly. I'm going to be taking care of her for a few weeks."

"Wow. That's a brave adventure. I've got just the thing a baby her age would love. But you'll need to break it up into small pieces." Amanda moved off and came back shortly with a glazed donut. "Just do yourself a favor and use the high chair to keep her sticky fingers away from your outfit. You're dressed up mighty fine to be playing mommy." Amanda shook her head and laughed.

"Actually, I start a new job in Lancaster today. Faith is meeting me and is going to look after Holly during the day when I work." At least she hoped her sister would show up. Based on her sister's track record and how late she was right now, things weren't looking good.

"Sounds like you got everything under control. What can I get you this morning?"

"I think Faith is partial to your custard-filled chocolate-covered doughnuts, so I'll take two of those. And maybe another glazed donut. For me, I'd like an old-fashioned one. Oh, and two cups of coffee, please."

The door opened and closed, the overhead bell jingling to announce a new customer. Grace glanced up, fully expecting to see Faith. It wasn't her. It was a handsome man, and she couldn't help but do a double-take before he came up behind her and stood in line. It would look odd if she turned around now to check him out, so she stilled the driving need to see if he looked as good up close as he had across the room.

Dressed in a suit and tie, he looked a little out of place for the Hallbrook bakery and was no one she'd seen before, earmarking him as an out-of-towner. He was probably just passing through and needed coffee. He'd picked an excellent place to stop, considering Amanda's sweet treats were known throughout the county.

Amanda returned to the counter with everything Grace had ordered and set them down on the tray to ring up the bill.

"Oh, sorry. But can you make that to go? I don't want to be late. I have no idea what's keeping Faith, but I'm going to wring her neck if she doesn't get here in the next few minutes."

"Will do. The baby's glazed donut is on me, so your total is $12.58," Amanda said.

"Thank you. That's very sweet." Grace shoved the diaper bag behind her. She concentrated on digging through her handbag to find the wallet buried deep within its depths. Holly fussed, reaching for the donuts as Amanda started to bag them. Grace bounced her on her hip as she struggled to find her wallet and kept coming up empty-handed.

She didn't remember throwing the wallet in the diaper bag. Still, she had to look, not sure if her frazzled nerves getting ready this morning had made her do something out of character. She swung the bag around front, letting it land on the counter next to her handbag. There wasn't much room to operate, and her search turned up with nothing. She tossed the diaper bag back to the ground and shifted Holly to the other side, her frustrated cries ringing in Grace's ears.

"I'm sorry," she said to the man behind her, shrugging as if it would explain everything. She dug to the bottom of her handbag again, finally locating her wallet and breathing a sigh of relief. Except her credit card wasn't where she usually put it, and she was out of cash. It wouldn't have been that bad if she hadn't thrown a bazillion last-minute things in the bag before she left this morning. Amanda returned with the two coffees, having put a lid on them and placed them in a cardboard carry tray.

"I'm sorry. My credit card has to be down in this bottomless pit somewhere. I'm getting there." Holly fussed louder, her cries becoming more concerning. Grace kept bouncing her gently in an effort to soothe the baby, all while she continued her search.

"You're fine." Amanda was trying to be sweet, but Grace noticed her gaze flicker to the man standing in line behind her. Where was Faith when she needed her? This was ridiculous. How did anybody find anything with one hand?

"Allow me," the man behind her spoke, offering his credit card.

"That's very kind of you, but it's not necessary. I've got this. I swear, I've got this. Just give me a second."

The man's expression revealed his irritation, but he dropped his hand.

Holly let out a piercing scream. "*Shhhh*, Holly. Please." Grace shifted the baby to the other side and used her other hand to dig through her handbag, trying to feel the loose card by touch. Tampon. Kleenex. Earrings. Hairbrush. Receipt. Lipstick. *Come on, where are you?* She'd fallen into the trap like a lot of women, carrying their lives with them in the precious depths of what should've been termed a suitcase rather than a handbag.

"Can I get half a dozen jelly-filled donuts, half a dozen glazed donuts, half a dozen chocolate-covered donuts, and half a dozen scones, please? And a cup of coffee. To go. Perhaps you could work on that while she locates her money. I'm in a hurry," he added, the irritation in his voice sliding into overdrive.

Amanda nodded." Not a problem, sir."

Grace looked back at him. "I'm sorry. I don't know what's wrong with the baby. It's hard to juggle her and everything else, especially when she's screaming," Grace offered by way of apology.

"Do you need help? Is there something I can find for you?" The man offered, but his expression made it clear it was more of a rhetorical question and not an actual offer.

There was no way she'd let him paw through her handbag. Not with her stash of feminine products floating around in there. That would be mortifying. But an extra set of hands with the baby would be a big help. Grace eyed the man up and down, trying to make a snap character assessment. She learned to trust her judgment years ago and he seemed like a good guy. Short on patience, maybe, but still a good guy.

"Would you mind holding Holly?" She held the baby out as if it were a foregone conclusion he would help. Who didn't like to hold babies? And he had offered his assistance, just not in the exact way she needed.

"You're serious?" The man's shocked expression would be almost laughable if it weren't for Holly's crying. She didn't know what was wrong with the baby.

"Please. I need to find the baby's paci and my credit card."

Ryan didn't have a clue what a paci was, but if it would stop the baby's crying, he was all for it. The baby screamed as if in pain, and there was no way Ryan wanted to hold her. He looked for help, but the place was empty. Figures. Since when was a bakery practically deserted this early in the morning?

He let out a deep breath. "Umm, okay." He reached out for the little girl and held her away from him, unsure exactly what was expected. Ryan glanced behind the counter, praying his order would be ready soon and he could extradite himself from this daymare. At least in a nightmare you could wake up and it would be over, but this wouldn't go away if he closed his eyes and reopened them.

The pretty woman dug through the oversized bag she'd previously tossed on the floor.

"I got it!" she exclaimed, a smile on her face as she looked up at him, holding up some plastic miracle gadget. For a brief second, he was lost in her joy, at least until the baby cried out again.

Ryan lowered his arms a bit, preparing to hand the baby back to her, but he suddenly found himself doused with white projectile vomit. It smelled like foul milk of the worst kind. The daymare had just gotten worse.

"Oh, my gosh, I'm so sorry. The poor baby. I don't know what's wrong. She did drink her milk awfully fast this morning." Grace took Holly from the man and hugged the little girl with zero regard of the mess she was making of her pink sweater. The baby settled down almost instantly when the woman put the plastic thing in her mouth and rested her head against the woman's shoulder. It was a sweet picture. Mother and daughter.

And a far cry from the torment of seconds ago. The woman grabbed a handful of napkins from the counter and started to wipe at his jacket, reminding him of the mess.

Ryan grabbed her arm and stopped her. "Please, don't. Just take care of the baby. I've got this." He tried to maintain control over his emotions, realizing getting angry would only make things worse. It wasn't the woman's fault.

If anything, he felt a twinge of sympathy for her. Kids were chaotic, and that was one of the reasons he never planned to have any of his own. Kids and family were trouble with a capital T. He wiped at his suit, doing the best he could. It would have to be dry cleaned, or maybe thrown out. It could be added to the pile of ruined clothing he'd started this morning when he'd burned the first shirt he tried to iron, which was the whole reason he was running late in the first place.

The woman was close to tears, and the last thing he wanted to deal with right now was someone having a mental breakdown. The baby was more than enough. The server behind the counter returned with his order.

Ryan reached for it and tossed a fifty on the counter. "That should cover my tab and hers. Keep the change." He nodded in the mother's direction and headed for the door, not bothering to wait for an answer.

It was a good thing his partner wasn't in town, or he'd never hear the end of it. Late and smelling like vomit was not exactly the professional image he aimed for as an example to his employees. As far as mornings were concerned, this one took the cake. Or the donut, in this case. Good thing it couldn't get any worse.

Chapter Three

♥

"Nice man," Amanda said, shooting Grace a wink.

"Among other things." She shrugged, not sure what to make of him. She was grateful the baby seemed to be feeling better, even if it had been at the man's expense. He'd gone before she could thank him, but then who could blame the guy? All in all, he'd taken getting thrown up on by a stranger's baby well. She glanced at her phone to check the time just as it rang.

Faith.

Twenty minutes late, her sister better have a darn good excuse. The morning was already a disaster, and Grace was going to be late for her first day on the job if she didn't leave in the next five minutes.

"Where are you?" she demanded, skipping any civil greetings.

"Lighten up, sis. I was out late last night, and I slept in." Faith yawned loudly.

"But I needed you here. You promised." Grace shifted the baby to her other hip, holding her close and trying to keep her calm. The last thing she needed right now was for the baby to pick up on her agitation and start fussing again, or worse, throw up on *her* this time.

"I know, and I'm sorry. But you did hit me up at the last minute, and you didn't give me much chance to think of what it would mean. The thing is, now that I've thought about it, I don't think it's such a good idea."

"What are you talking about? You can't change your mind now. Don't do this to me, Faith." Grace closed her eyes, taking in a deep breath. Everything in her life was spinning out of control, but she only had herself to blame. She should have never trusted her sister, and she should have never said yes to Karen in the first place. It had just been too good of an opportunity to pass up. But now, less than twenty-four hours later, it was turning out to be nothing short of a disastrous decision.

"I'm not ready for a full-time job. Especially not as a babysitter." Faith still wasn't ready to grow up and accept the fact she was an adult, which meant living in the real world with a job and paying bills. And if her mother continued to baby her, she'd never mature, that much was obvious.

Grace had no one else she could turn to at the last minute and wasn't above begging. "You were okay with it last night. Please, Faith."

"Well, the thing is, that was before the gang talked about taking a road trip. My plans have changed."

"I was counting on you. What am I supposed to do now?" Her sister was totally bailing on her. They'd never been close, the age difference between them always a problem, amongst other things.

"I said I was sorry. You are the one who got yourself into this. I'm sure you'll figure a way out. You always do." Grace could hear the resentment in her sister's voice. Sure, she'd done well in high school and then in college, but it was because she applied herself. It's not like it came easy. It wasn't her fault

Faith had no such aspirations and fell short of the standards Grace had set.

Her mother harped on her sister's shortcomings, often comparing the two sisters as a method of motivation. In the end, it always backfired. And then her mother would jump through hoops to make things right with Faith. She almost felt sorry for her sister. Almost. Right now, Grace was mad at her.

"You realize, of course, you may have just cost me my new job. Thanks a lot." Grace hung up on her sister. Maybe it had been unfair to spring the offer on Faith, but no one had forced her sister to accept. And it was Faith's promise to watch Holly during the day that had prompted Grace's acceptance to keep the baby for a few weeks.

She tried to think of who she could call. Olivia, her best friend, worked during the day and had her hands full with her own twins. On such short notice, there wasn't anyone she could think of who would be available that she could trust or keep up with a crawling baby. And if Grace called out of work on her first day, she'd get fired. If she showed up at the office with Holly, she'd probably lose her job regardless of the circumstances. But the word *probably* was enough to get her in the car and driving toward Lancaster.

The country landscape that typically brought her peace as she drove to the city failed to capture her attention. There was no way this would end well, but she had to try. "It's just you and me, kiddo," she said, glancing in the rearview mirror and talking to Holly, who'd fallen asleep in her car seat. "Let's just hope the new boss is an understanding guy. The last thing I want to do is give up my independence and move back home because I can't make ends meet."

Grace followed the GPS directions and pulled into the parking lot of the enormous warehouse where her office was located. Lots of cars filled the first several rows of spaces, leaving her to park farther away than she liked considering the load she had to carry.

She stepped out of the car and glanced down at her outfit, disgusted with what she saw. So much for professionalism. Wrinkled and stained, the image she'd gone for, all but shot. Grace gently took Holly out of her seat, trying not to wake her considering the baby had just fallen asleep. Grabbing the blanket, the baby bag, and her handbag in the other hand, she made her way to the entrance. Overloaded, she was relieved when a young man opened the door for her, but she could do without his are-you-from-outer-space look.

"Thanks," she said, more to the man's back as he took off down the hall, as if in a hurry. Grace had no idea where to go, and she was already late. "Excuse me," she called after him.

The man paused, one hand on the door he was about to go through and turned back toward her.

"Do you know where the welcome meeting is being held?" Grace shifted the diaper bag and handbag straps up to her shoulder, trying to balance some of the weight.

"You mean the one that started fifteen minutes ago? It's this way." The guy jerked his thumb toward the door he was standing in front of. "This is the warehouse. Good luck."

Good luck not being fired for being late on your first day, or good luck not being fired for bringing your kid to work? It didn't matter which one, because either way, she needed all the luck she could get.

Grace shifted the sleeping baby in her arms and pushed through the swinging door. A large group of people stood not far from the entrance, all gathered around to listen to whoever was talking in front of them. Moving slowly, she eased toward the back of the group, hoping to join in without a disturbance.

"May I help you?" a man asked the question, his voice somewhat familiar.

Grace cringed, terrified he was talking to her. She tried to duck behind the woman in front of her, hoping to get lost in the crowd, and keeping Holly hidden. For now.

"May I help you," he asked again. "I'm talking to the person at the back of the room who just walked in this meeting late. What's your name? I don't tolerate tardiness, and on the first day no less, it shows a lack of respect for your employer." The man's crisp, business-like tone made her feel like she was in the principal's office in high school.

"I'm sorry. My name is Grace Baxter, and I start work here today." This was a bad idea. She should've never come. "I ran into trouble. I promise it won't happen again."

"See that it doesn't." The bright light made it hard for her to make out the man. His voice, however, was very clear. The guy wasn't happy with her first-day performance, and he didn't even know the worst yet—she'd brought a baby to work. She was as good as fired if he reported her to the bosses.

The man continued to address the group, explaining company policy and rules and expectations. Grace only heard half of it. His voice was driving her crazy as she tried to remember where she'd heard it before. She inched her way around the outside edge of the group, trying to move closer to get a good look at him.

He was tall, had brown wavy hair, and an athletic build. The man was dressed in a long-sleeved dress shirt and dark dress pants. He turned toward her, and instant recognition slammed into Grace.

Vomit Man. Grace sucked in a deep breath. Her odds of not getting fired had just dropped to none. Just when she thought the morning couldn't get any worse, it had. She started to edge her way to the back of the room, determined to save face.

A horn blasted from somewhere on the side of the room, startling Grace and Holly. The baby cried out; her eyes wide open with fear as she looked around.

"Stop!" Vomit Man hollered; his booming voice unmistakable now.

Grace froze. The crowd parted as he made his way through the crowd. She knew the minute he recognized her. The deep lines on his forehead were a quick tell it wasn't going to be a happy reunion.

"You! What are you doing here? Did you come back for round two or something?" His sarcastic comment was uncalled for and put Grace more on the defensive than was merited given the circumstances.

"No. I'm here to do my job." She could feel a warm flush on her cheeks and throat as blood rushed to the areas, her usual confidence shaken.

"Your job? You must be in the wrong place." He flicked a glance down at Holly, dismissing her comment completely.

"Or not. Jordan Tate hired me," she said, holding her chin high, unwilling to be browbeaten for a situation out of her control.

"What did you say your name is?" His gaze drilled her with its intensity, the lines on his forehead deepening if it were possible.

"Grace Baxter. Mr. Walker's new assistant." She spoke up, unwilling to back down under his inspection. She was very good at her job. Hopefully, she'd get a chance to prove it. And the baby was only a minor temporary setback. Being cowardly wouldn't get her that chance, and she had nothing to lose.

"My assistant?" He glanced down at the clipboard he held and shook his head, running a hand through his hair.

My assistant. The words took a second to register. Vomit Man was her new boss. Oh, yeah, the day had just become the worst day of her life.

"There must be a mistake. We don't allow children at work. We have no daycare facility. Jordan may have hired you, but I'm not sure this is a good match. I need to finish up this meeting, and then you and I need to talk. Please, wait in my office. When you leave here, go back down the hall, and it's the first office on your right." He wasn't giving her a choice in the matter, whether he used the word please or not. The man was used to people obeying his orders.

"Yes, Mr. Walker. I'm sorry if you think there's been a misunderstanding. Hopefully, we can work this out," she aimed for civility, keeping tight control over every word she uttered.

"Not likely." Vomit Man didn't have the same problem.

It felt as though her heart had dropped into her stomach. Every shred of hope vanished. She turned and walked out the way she'd come, glad to be away from the crowd and her new boss. *At least he was for the next few minutes.*

Holly was usually a good baby. The tummy ache and rude awakening that caused her to fuss and cry out weren't the norms, but Vomit Man wouldn't care about any of that. Grace glanced at the exit door, tempted to just keep walking. What was the use of sticking around to hear him tell her she was fired? Talk about pouring salt on a wound.

She glanced down at the baby and held her close. "We've come this far, might as well hear what he has to say. I've never turned tail and run from any-thing, and I don't intend to start now, no matter how tempting. Plus, it will give me the chance to thank him for paying for breakfast. What do you say, Holly?" The baby gurgled, a smile puffing up her chubby cheeks.

The decision was made, now all that was left was to wait for the guillotine to fall.

Ryan found it difficult to concentrate through the rest of the meeting after coming face-to-face with the woman from this morning. A walking disaster if there ever was one. He brought this part of the orientation to a conclusion.

"Everyone take a fifteen-minute break and meet me back here for a tour of the plant. I'll take questions after the tour." The new group of employees started to disperse, the noise level in the room rising as people began getting to know one another.

As for him, he had more important things to do than idol chat. He needed to get rid of the woman in his office. But there was one major problem with what he wanted to do and what needed to be done. With the grand opening of World Sport Inc. in a week, he'd never find anyone with her qualifications on such short notice based on Jordan's glowing praise of the woman. Smart. Determined. Creative. Experienced.

Of course, Jordan also mentioned she was attractive, not that it had any bearing on her qualifications for the job. But at no point had his business partner mentioned a baby. There was no way his friend knew this woman intended to bring her daughter to work. Jordan may have gotten it right on all the other points, but it didn't make Grace Baxter the right candidate.

He walked into his office and drew up short, the scene in front of him like something out of a reality TV show. Grace sat on her knees playing with the baby, toys spread out on a blanket in the corner. Grace's sweet laughter filled the room before she realized he was standing behind her. A woman in her position had nothing to laugh about, and yet the baby had no trouble making her do just that.

Grace immediately schooled her expression into one of professionalism, coming to her feet in a hurry. Her hair had come free of the bun, and blonde tendrils curled loosely around her shoulders. Her outfit had seen better days, the wrinkles and stains marking her as a mother.

But then he wasn't exactly the epitome of professionalism himself, having lost his jacket and tie to the same now-laughing baby this morning. "Let's cut the bull and get this over with, shall we?" He moved to sit behind his desk.

"I understand, Mr. Walker. I do. But please, give me a chance to explain." She approached, hands on her hips, facing off with him with a level of confidence he hadn't expected for a woman in her situation.

"I'm not sure there's any explanation that could change this situation. This is a workplace, and although I'm sure there's nothing in the employee manual that states you can't bring a baby to work, I'm sure it's implied. This is a large warehouse with machines and vehicles moving inventory, not a child's play place. This is a new business, and the launch is very important to me. I need a dedicated team that can do the job they were hired for. And nowhere in your job description did it include childcare."

Ryan leaned back in his seat, running his hands through his hair in frustration. Firing her might be a more costly option at this point if he applied the risk-reward assessment he liked to use to substantiate his decisions. If he fired her, they would have zero ads ready for the launch, and the start-up would be doomed to failure. If he kept her, they might get some ads, which would be better than nothing at this point.

"I'm sorry. You're right. But my sister was supposed to watch the baby. She's nineteen, got a better offer, and ditched me. She's who I was waiting for at the bakery this morning. Which, by the way, I'm very sorry about Holly, umm, you know, umm, throwing up on you." Grace winced. "Holly drank her milk fast this morning. Maybe with all the excitement, it gave her an upset tummy. I think that's why she was crying because she was fine after she, umm, threw up. She's a good baby, I promise. Look," Grace said, pointing at the little girl. "She can sit in the corner and play. It's just for today."

Ryan was all too familiar with being ditched by a sister. Grace's words reminded him of his own sister and her betrayal. It softened his heart just enough that he was relieved he hadn't come in guns blazing and fired her on the spot as he would have preferred to do. *And it is only for today.*

It would be foolish to lose an employee that came this highly qualified over a one-day situation. He wasn't a total ogre. "So this isn't something you plan to do every day?" he asked for clarification. Maybe there was a silver lining in this disaster.

So far, he'd seen nothing but the scatterbrained mother skills, but he trusted his partner's judgment. Not to mention, he needed Grace as his assistant. He might be good at business dealings, but he wasn't good at designing marketing ad campaigns or setting up an online presence. A marketing genius was precisely what they needed to get this new sporting goods company off the ground, putting them in direct competition with the largest online retailer in the country. Other than a few small locations scattered across the country at various ski resorts, they'd have no brick-and-mortar presence.

"Just for today—I think. I don't make promises I can't keep. My intentions weren't to bring Holly to work now or in the future. I will do everything in my power to find a sitter, so this doesn't happen again."

Ryan let out a deep breath. Grace looked up at him, her beautiful blue eyes imploring him to give her a chance. He gazed down at Holly, who smiled at him, the simple action melting his resistance just enough for him to decide.

"Fine. One day. Your office is across the hall from mine. I left you a packet that explains your passcodes and usernames. You can use the day to get familiar with our programs. I'll be around after I lead the other employees through the tour of the warehouse. If you have any questions, jot them down, and we can go over them later. And keep the baby out of the warehouse." He was out of his mind, but it's not like he had a choice. World Sport Inc. needed Grace Baxter. Letting her know how much, on the other hand, would be a mistake.

"You won't regret this, I promise," Grace said, her smile revealing perfectly formed dimples.

"I hope you're right. But understand, this is a conditional continuation of your employment."

"Yes, sir." Grace bent down to retrieve the toys and stuff them in the diaper bag.

"Ryan." He nodded. "If we're going to be working together, we should be on a first-name basis." It was a courtesy he extended all employees, not just pretty women and children.

"Thank you, Ryan. Holly and I appreciate this," Grace said, picking up the baby and heading for the door.

He glanced at his watch and stood. It was time for the warehouse tour and time for Grace to prove she could do her job with a baby in tow.

"Let me know if you need anything." His new assistant just bought herself twenty-four hours. Ryan could only hope Grace was right, and he didn't regret his decision.

Chapter Four

♥

GRACE ENTERED HER NEW office and set Holly down. She laid the blanket and toys back on the carpeted floor and placed the baby right in the middle with hopes she'd play for a while and then sleep. Luckily, Karen kept emergency food in the diaper bag, so Grace was good for meals and milk for the rest of the day. The shredded donut she fed Holly this morning wasn't exactly a nutritious start.

She gazed around the room, picking up and moving anything that could prove problematic for a baby. "You be a good girl and play. You need to be on your best behavior, so the mean old boss won't fire me." Grace chuckled, knowing Holly didn't understand a word of what she was saying. The baby reached for a toy and held it up for Grace's inspection. Toys were much more important than words. The little girl smiled and banged it on the floor, and the toy came alive with music.

Grabbing for the toy, she glanced at the door, hoping no one heard. She searched for the button to shut it off, sliding the black knob to the right. The office immediately returned to its golden silence. "Maybe you can play with it in quiet mode," she encouraged Holly as she handed her back the toy.

Satisfied, Grace sat down at her desk and powered up the computer. Using the information Ryan left her, she managed to log in with no issue. She clicked on the World Sport Inc. icon and several files popped up. One by one, Grace opened them, trying to do a general review. The two she was most concerned with were the Excel spreadsheet used for keeping up with the sales numbers, and of course, her specialty, the ad design software.

Every few minutes, Grace glanced over at Holly, grateful the little girl was playing happily and quietly. She watched her for a few minutes, fascinated by the little things that held the baby's interest. Something as simple as a star or a triangle of a different color could prompt a child to investigate.

Grace smiled and forced her attention back to the spreadsheets.

She reviewed the ads the partners had drafted for the grand opening next week. They weren't bad, but they weren't creative. It did, however, give her an idea of what they were looking for. Grace clicked on the first ad and started to play with some of the tools available, trying out various ideas. The more she clicked and added, the more she thought about what she could do to enhance the ad and make it pop.

Lost deep in thought, Grace was startled by a banging noise. She glanced up to discover Holly pounding on the wall with her blocks. Grace got up and brought the baby back to the blanket. "Play with your toys right here, honey."

Grace went back to her desk and tried to refocus. This time, however, she attempted to keep a better eye on Holly. The baby had decided the blanket wasn't the end of her play-place world. She felt like a Jack-in-the-Box trying to keep up with the active crawler in exploration mode.

Twenty minutes later, a crashing noise caught her attention, Grace jumping to her feet. The baby had crawled under a chair in the corner of the office, knocking the plastic holder filled with brochures onto the ground from the table next to it. Leaflets had gone every which way creating a sea of brochures. Holly lost no time and began using her hands and feet to scramble them like eggs. The baby seemed completely satisfied for the moment, and Grace opted to return to her seat. The brochures could be replaced, and the baby was having fun. Which also meant, Grace could keep working.

She focused on the finishing touches for the first ad, pleased with the results. At least when Mr. Walker—Ryan, that is—returned, Grace would have something to show for her time. Proof she could manage both the baby, her job, and her life. Something that so far, was a side she hadn't shown him.

Images of the morning disaster danced through her head, causing her to cringe all over again. Maybe it would be better if she told Ryan the truth, that Holly wasn't hers, and that the whole baby duty was temporary. It might alleviate his concerns about her ability to do the job going forward. But then there was a concern he might land on the other side of the spreadsheet.

The side that wouldn't appreciate her taking on a situation of this magnitude the day before she started a new job. He might consider that irresponsible, which would put her in a worse light. It was one thing for him to think Holly was hers and she had no choice, quite another to realize this was a mess she'd created.

It wasn't a chance she could take. She needed this job, and all she had to do was get through today, and then Ryan wouldn't be able to find fault with anything she did. Provided, of course, she found childcare.

Holly started to fuss, her whimpering soft and somehow sweet. It was the sound of a baby that needed a little attention. Grace hit save on the ad she was working on and moved to pick up Holly from her island of brochures. Her outfit felt wet, a quick reminder Grace hadn't changed the baby all morning. *Rookie mistake.*

She grabbed the diaper bag and laid the baby down on the blanket to change her, grateful there were extra changes of clothes packed. Something else she needed to remember when she packed to go places—spare outfits. Two or three preferably.

"There you go, sweetheart. Don't cry. You're all dry now," Grace said, picking her up and giving her a kiss on the forehead. Holly continued to fuss, and Grace glanced nervously at the door, hoping Ryan wouldn't make an appearance. She looked up at the clock on the wall, disappointed to realize it was only eleven o'clock. *Talk about a slow day.*

Grace wondered if the baby needed to eat again. Karen hadn't given her a feeding schedule before she'd rushed off to be with the band. Totally irresponsible, reminding Grace all too much of her sister. She couldn't imagine Faith taking care of a baby at this stage of her life, and yet that's exactly what she'd asked her sister to do. Except she asked Faith to babysit, not become a full-time mom. Her cousin hadn't been ready to be a mom, either, but she'd been blessed with a baby. It was a shame Karen didn't focus on the joy of having Holly in her life.

Grace hugged the baby close, hoping to settle her down. When that didn't work, she laid her on the blanket and then began searching the diaper bag for a bottle and the can of powdered milk. After reading the back of the cannister to refresh her memory from this morning, she carefully measured out the powder. Grace picked up Holly, putting her on one hip, while she grabbed up the bottle, and went in search of water.

The fountain she'd spotted earlier in the hallway would do the trick. Luckily, it seemed Holly was past the warm-milk stage. It might have been next to impossible to accommodate that on such short notice. The baby instantly stopped crying when she spotted Grace filling the bottle, her chubby little hands reaching for it before it was full.

Grace laughed and handed her the bottle. "Just don't drink it as fast as you did this morning, or we're both in trouble again. We can't afford a re-peat." Back in her office, Grace scrunched the soft, fuzzy blanket on one side into a pillow. She laid Holly back against it, the baby content to hold her own bottle as she drank.

Did one-year-olds need to be burped? Grace hadn't burped her this morning, and maybe, that's what sent everything into a tailspin.

Grace returned to her desk, keeping a closer watch on Holly's progress, waiting to see if she slowed down or got to the halfway point. It wasn't long before the baby started pulling the bottle out of her mouth, and then sticking it back in, only suckling a few times before she repeated the pattern. *Was that the sign?*

After closing the screen on her computer, Grace went and sat next to Holly on the blanket. She picked up the baby, held her to her chest, and patted her back gently. Almost instantly, Holly let out a long burp. "Goodness, gracious." Grace smiled. She continued to pat Holly's back a few more times, but when nothing happened, she laid her down and gave her the bottle. "Does that feel better, honey?"

The baby made babbling noises right before she stuck the bottle in her mouth. Comfortable Holly would remain occupied for a few minutes, Grace returned to her desk and pulled up the ad she'd been working on.

Glancing up every now and then to make sure Holly was okay, she noticed the baby's eyes drooping. It wasn't long before Holly was fast asleep. The bottle had rolled out of her mouth and lay off to the side. There was no way Grace was waking the baby to burp her. This was her first moment of down-time, and she intended to get a lot accomplished.

The door opened, Ryan filling the doorway as he stepped inside. "I'm just checking—"

Grace quickly put a finger to her lips to indicate for him to keep his voice down as she pointed at the baby.

"Gotcha," he said in a lower voice, mindful of her warning. "I just wanted to see how you are making out."

"Everything's fine. I've almost finished redesigning the first ad. I think you'll really like it." She smiled at Ryan, hoping to ease the tension between them from earlier this morning. As far as first impressions went, hers had been dismally lacking.

"Let's hope your ad designs are more creative than the baby's." His gaze slid to the brochures on the floor.

Grace wasn't sure if he was amused or angry, his stoic expression unreadable. "I'm sorry. Holly was having so much fun, I let her play so I could keep working. I can pay for the brochures if you need me to."

"That won't be necessary. It's just unexpected, much the same way as having a baby in the office in the first place. I'll be across the hall if you need anything."

"Thank you. And thank you for not firing me on the spot. You won't regret it," she said as he turned to leave.

"Let's hope not." Ryan left, closing the door firmly behind him. It was comforting to know the baby was sleeping while Ryan was in his office. There would be little chance of her disturbing him.

Grace hit send on the first ad, emailing it to Ryan for approval. She was anxious to work on the second ad but opted instead to get familiar with the daily sales register reports that would be sent over from the accounting office. Once World Sport Inc. opened their doors for business, she'd be responsible for compiling all the weekly, monthly, and annual sales reports—that is, if she lasted that long.

Everything was laid out in a logical way, which would make her job easier. The fact they wanted it broken down by various regions made it more difficult, but it was nothing she couldn't handle. Hopefully, it wouldn't be long before they were able to hire a separate office administrator so she could focus on her one true love. *Marketing*.

Grace pulled up the second ad but found it hard to concentrate, preferring to watch Holly as she slept. It was only Monday, but she was already looking forward to the weekend. A time when she'd have all day to revel in the joy of having a baby with her. Not just at night after work, but two whole days. The park would be a fun place to take Holly, or maybe a walk around town to show her off. They could watch videos or simply play on the floor.

An email popped into Grace's account, the notification icon flashing with a big red number one to announce her unread email count. She typed in the username and password provided in her new employee paperwork.

Incorrect username or password.

Passwords were always frustrating, the stars to protect the privacy providing no help as to whether the account holder typed the word correctly the first time around. Grace retyped the information.

Incorrect username or password.

She glanced at Holly and then at her door. Ryan had said to ask if she needed help, and it would seem she did. There was always a chance the password he'd provided was wrong, or the account wasn't set up properly.

Coming to a decision, she headed for Ryan's office after one last check on Holly. Grace would only be gone for a few seconds, and if she left the door open, she'd know if the baby woke up.

Grace tapped the door before entering his office to announce her arrival, even though it was wide open. He glanced up at her, pausing over whatever document he was working on.

"Do you need something?" he asked, getting straight to the point.

"Yes. The password on my email account isn't working." She shrugged.

"Have you tried it a couple of times to make sure you input it correctly? They are case sensitive." He frowned, sitting back in his chair, resigned to deal with the problem.

"This isn't my first rodeo using an email, and, yes, I've tried several times." She couldn't help the sarcasm that tinged her voice, but it was no more than he deserved.

"Hang on, and I'll check it out," Ryan said, frustration evident in every word. He closed the file on his desk and placed it in his top drawer. He stood and crossed the room, following her across the hall.

Grace glanced at Holly as she entered her office, relieved the baby was still sound asleep. She sat at her desk, while Ryan moved to stand behind her, looking over her shoulder to see the screen. His cologne wafted around her, the spicy musk appealing. She didn't want to think of him as anything other than her boss, but this close, she couldn't help her wandering brain. Strangely enough, he made her nervous. Giddy, to be exact.

Except giddy was for young girls and lovesick fools, and she was neither.

Ryan reached down in front of her as she leaned back and let him take control of the computer. He typed in her username and then the passcode on the form.

Incorrect username and password.

"Told you. Either the information is wrong, or you're no better at this than I am," Grace teased, challenging Ryan on his earlier comments.

"Very funny. I didn't mean anything by it, it's just the typical first question anybody asks when a password doesn't work. And it's the same question the IT guy will ask me when I call him."

There was some definite truth to what Ryan said. "Point taken," Grace conceded.

Ryan pulled his phone from his pocket, pressed a few buttons, and waited. He'd put it on speakerphone, but at least it wasn't set to a high volume.

She glanced nervously at Holly, but so far, the baby hadn't stirred.

"John Baden. How can help you?" the man asked, getting straight to the point.

"Hey, John, it's Ryan. We're having trouble logging in on Grace Baxter's email account."

"The passwords are case sensitive. Did you make sure to retype it with the correct upper and lower cases?"

Ryan shot her an I-told-you-so look. "I have, multiple times, in fact. Can you connect and see what's going on?"

"Sure thing. Hang on." Within seconds, John connected to her computer, taking over the control from his remote location.

Ryan glanced at the sleeping baby and then back at her. He pressed the mute button. "She's been asleep a long time. Is that normal?" He frowned.

"Yes." At least she assumed it was. It's not like she was an expert.

"Good way for you to get your work done." Was Ryan trying to make amends for his earlier gruffness?

"I'm not accomplishing anything right now, and it's no fault of Holly's," she teased, taking his moment of weakness and making the most of it.

"Point taken," he said, mocking her words.

John moved her mouse pointer across the screen and tapped her email icon. He typed in her password, except this time, her account opened instantly. "There doesn't seem to be a problem now. What username and password did you use?"

Ryan unmuted the phone and read back the information from the paperwork.

"Well, there's your problem. The password is World12B, not World12D. B as in Baxter. That's how we set up all the emails."

"Gotcha. I'll remember that in the future. Thanks," Ryan said, picking up a pen and changing it on her paperwork.

"No problem."

After the two men hung up, Ryan glanced at her, his expression apologetic. "Sorry. I copied it wrong."

"No worries. Apparently, we are all human and can make mistakes. Just keep that in mind, boss." She grinned.

Ryan caught and held her gaze as if unsure what to say. Seconds passed before he finally nodded. "I'll do that." He left her office without another word, leaving Grace to wonder more and more about the man, and not necessarily as her boss.

The email turned out to be nothing more than a welcome letter, and soon, she was back working on the second ad. The shrill tone of an incoming call on her cell phone had her scrambling to silence it.

Faith.

Grace debated whether to answer, still upset with her sister for the predicament she was in today and for the rest of the week. She may have told Ryan it was one day, but it would only be one day if she could find somebody else to watch Holly on short notice.

"Hello?" Grace said in hushed tones, worried the call would rouse the baby. Every second Holly slept was valuable work time.

"It's me, Faith."

"I realize that. What's going on? I've got work to do." Grace didn't have time for more of her sister's nonsense.

"I've called to tell you I've changed my mind. I'll watch Holly like I promised." Except Faith didn't sound overly happy with the decision, and therefore, it wasn't something Grace could put stock in.

She wouldn't play this game again with her sister. "I don't know. You put me in a difficult position this morning by bagging out on me. And you don't sound all that excited about it now. What gives?"

"Mom. I'm not gonna lie, I'd rather be out having fun. And babysitting doesn't ring any fun bells for me."

"What does Mom have to do with this?" Grace asked.

"Apparently, everything. Mom found out from Aunt Judith that you were watching the baby, and she asked me if I knew anything about it. I made the mistake of telling her you'd asked me to babysit. One thing led to another, and I was told in no uncertain terms that if I didn't help you out and then get a full-time job afterward, I'm going to need to find a new place to live. Apparently, she doesn't believe kids should have fun for a little while after thirteen years of being a prisoner in the school system," Faith said sourly.

"The problem is, Faith, you're not a kid. You're a young woman now. The time for all-day fun was while you were in school. Now it's time to become responsible for yourself. Lay the groundwork and be like any other normal adult. You must work to earn money, get a place of your own, become your own person. Then you get to make your own rules. If you're living at home, you play by Mom's rules."

Grace was happy her mother was finally bringing the situation to a head. Her sister had been ruled by fun for far too long and showed no signs of changing. Something had to give.

"What about fun?" Faith asked petulantly.

"Welcome to adulthood. You must work to make money, pay bills, and when you can fit it in, have fun. It's simple. Time to grow up, sis."

"Whatever. I don't have to like it, but I'll do it. I'll be there in the morning. It sounds like I don't have a choice." Taking Faith at her word was difficult at best, or stupidity at its worst.

"Promise?" Grace hoped she wouldn't regret the decision, but it's not like she had many choices.

"Promise."

Ryan returned to his office and tried to focus on the file he had in front of him. Reading through some of the investors' concerns and suggestions, he wanted to give each one his personal attention and honest assessment. It was essential to keep them happy. After all, without the investors, he wouldn't have been able to put this grand plan for World Sport, Inc. into place. He'd personally sunk his life savings into the deal, but with the investors backing him, he'd been able to think big.

Globally big. Competing with the number one online retailer and trying to take their sporting goods business was a huge endeavor. It was a small piece of the internet pie, but it was a piece that would make a big difference to the sports enthusiasts of the world. World Sport would be a place they could get unparalleled technical support to have the confidence they were getting the right equipment based on skill, experience, and need. This type of in-depth technical support was nothing a huge online conglomerate could ever provide, and it would make World Sport a favorite.

Which is precisely why the situation with Grace irritated him. Everything he owned was riding on this company's success, and yet, one of the lead people in the organization had a baby. *At work.*

Ryan had always known family got in the way of business, and the two never mixed. His own parents were proof of that. His father had spent every waking moment taking care of his business, his wife, and his family. But in the end, his efforts hadn't been enough to save any of it.

But where his mother was soft and weak, Grace was determined and strong, surprising Ryan. Her down-home freshness had caught him off guard. He'd expected someone more city savvy with the experience listed on her resume. Ryan admired the realness of her attitude and her ability to meet life's challenges head-on without backing down. It would stand her in good stead throughout life, he just preferred those qualities weren't tested on his company. Or, at least, not against him.

He noticed she didn't wear a wedding band, which allowed him to make the leap that she was a single mom. Another piece of information he wished he didn't know, because it was one more reason he wouldn't fire her. He had a conscience, whether he approved of it or not. It was one of the big differences between him and his dad.

He pulled up the ad she'd emailed him, anxious to see what she'd come up with. Ryan wasn't disappointed. She'd nailed the exact attitude he was after. One-stop shopping and the go-to place for sports enthusiasts who cared to get their purchases right the first time around. He was excited by the spirit of the ad, and by her promise to have the video footage ready by the end of the week.

A movement at the door caught his attention. He was shocked to see the baby crawling toward him. Ryan didn't move, expecting at any moment to see Grace in hot pursuit to reclaim the errant wanderer.

Holly came right up to him, using his leg to hold on to as she pulled herself upright. It was a wobbly move at best, and Ryan reached out to steady the baby. "Grace," he called out.

The baby held up her arms, wanting to be picked up. Ryan debated what to do, hoping at any second Grace would appear. Holly started to babble small sounds, her smile tugging at his heartstrings.

"Hey there, Holly." He tentatively picked the baby up, almost afraid of a repeat performance of this morning. Except she was smiling, not crying. Ryan held her close, letting the baby pull at his tie and then poke his cheek with her chubby little finger. Ryan grinned.

"Don't tell your mom, but you are a cutie." A sensation of wetness crept through his shirt. Ryan looked down to see a dark-blue stain. The baby was soaked through and through. He held her away from him, unsure of what to do. First vomit, and now pee. The baby sure had a way of making sure he didn't form any attachment. If anything, it reinforced his mindset of never having children. This was disgusting.

Ryan waltzed into Grace's office, keeping the baby at arm's length.

She was hanging up the phone, which explained her lack of response—but not her lack of vigilance over her daughter. Grace glanced up, her expression turning to one of wide-eyed shock. Jumping up, she came around the desk, taking the baby from him. "What are you doing with Holly? I don't understand." Her gaze drifted to his shirt. "Oh, no. I'm sorry. She just woke up from her nap, and she's wet. You don't have much luck with babies, do you?" She grinned, her attempt to soften the situation falling short with him. She wasn't the one with a peed-on shirt.

"It would appear not. I thought we had an agreement that you were going to keep the baby in your office, which would require you to keep your door closed."

"I did. I don't know how it got opened." Grace shook her head, her brow pulled into a frown as she considered the situation.

"Well, it's safe to say she didn't open it." A sudden image of when he'd walked out of her office not long ago provided him with a good idea of what happened.

"But you did. And clearly, you didn't close it," Grace said, pointing out the same conclusion he'd come to.

"Fair enough." He shrugged. "I'll let this one pass. This isn't a lucky shirt for me and needs to be burned. It wouldn't be the first today," Ryan added, remembering his morning run in with another shirt before he'd even left the house.

Grace laid the baby down on the blanket and began changing her diaper. "Don't be so dramatic. The shirt just needs washing." She laughed. "And about the door, it's still my fault, and I didn't mean to imply otherwise. I'm not used to..." Grace stopped, leaving him to wonder what she'd been about to say. "I'm not used to having Holly in the office, and it's my responsibility to keep her contained and safe. My apologies. Send me the bill for the dry cleaning on the shirt."

"That won't be necessary." He was just ready for the day to be over.

"What did you mean about burning another shirt?" she asked.

He rolled his eyes. "I normally have everything dry cleaned, but Hallbrook doesn't have a dry cleaner. I tried to iron my shirt this morning and lost. The one I'm wearing was my second choice."

Grace laughed. "I see. You're a lot like Holly."

He wasn't sure he enjoyed being likened to a baby. "What do you mean?"

"You both require lots of clothing changes in a day. Perhaps you should keep extras around the way I do for the baby," she teased.

"At least I don't need a diaper change." He chuckled, seeing the humor in the situation for the first time. It was a one-off occurrence, and if anyone had told him this morning what his day would entail, he would have thought them insane. He didn't know how Grace did it on her own day after day, but he couldn't fault her sense of humor.

"There is that," she said, chuckling as she shot him a saucy grin. Grace picked up Holly and held her close. The image of a loving mother and daughter hit him hard. It wasn't anything he remembered growing up, at least not after he was placed in the foster system. And before that, his memories weren't that good either.

Ryan moved to leave, pausing at the door. "I'll close it this time. Out of curiosity, where's the baby's father?" He'd let the question slip before he had a chance to think better of it. There was no reason to get involved in an employee's personal life.

"I don't know. The father isn't interested in Holly." She shrugged as if it didn't matter. Maybe she was one of those independent women who wanted to raise a child on her own. More power to her if that was the case, if it didn't interfere with her ability to do her job.

"I see. You do have daycare for the rest of the week, right?"

"I do." Grace nodded with more assurance than when she'd spoken about the situation earlier today.

"Good. Tomorrow, we need to go to the Mt. Washington Ski Resort and check the setup and the inventory to make sure everything is ready for the grand opening. It's our only onsite location, and with it being off-season, they hope business will pick up for their summer sports."

"Sounds like fun. Should I meet you there?" Grace asked while getting the baby's bottle and formula out of the diaper bag, along with a jar of orange mush.

Ryan couldn't imagine anyone eating the stuff. "No. I'll pick you up. I live in Hallbrook, so it's easier to ride together."

"Since when? I'd never seen you until this morning at the bakery."

"Since yesterday." He laughed. "I was away on a business trip, which is why I wasn't able to be at the interview. I pre-arranged a place to stay in Hallbrook to force me to leave the warehouse and keep me from becoming a workaholic. It's one of the challenges I face."

"I see. That makes sense then," she said, nodding.

"Is nine okay?" Riding together would give him more time to get to know the woman he'd be working closely with, and for them to clear any remaining tension from the mishaps of today. It would be like a fresh start.

"That'll work." With one hand, she measured powder into the bottle, the baby in her other arm.

Apparently, her talents weren't limited to those they'd hired her for.

"I'll get your address from your employee file. If you need me for anything else today, call me on my cell phone. The number is in your paperwork. I'll be back in the warehouse and working with the employees for the rest of the afternoon."

"Gotcha." She put the plastic lid back on the can and tossed it in the bag.

"Oh, and one other thing. Nice work on the first ad you sent me. I put my seal of approval on it already." That should go a long way to making amends with her. After all, he'd been tough on her this morning.

"I'm glad you liked it. And thanks for the care package." Grace smiled, following him out of the office.

"Care package?" he asked.

"The baby. Care package. Get it?" She laughed. "Don't worry about the door, I've got to get water for her bottle."

"Gotcha." He winked and then headed down the hall, resisting the urge to turn around and walk with her. Grace was quite the woman, and he looked forward to seeing more of her. Professionally, of course.

Chapter Five

♥

GRACE WAS THRILLED WHEN the rest of the day went without incident. In fact, she hadn't even seen Ryan since Holly peed on him. Poor guy. It was obvious he wasn't a fan of kids, and Holly had done nothing to change his mind.

Ready to be home, she wished she could just skip the stop at the drug store, but her list was too long and too important to blow off the way she would have if it had only been her affected by the decision. Holly needed baby food, formula, and diapers, and Grace needed a baby monitor. It was easier to stock up on inventory rather than take the chance of running out. Based on how much powder went into each bottle, the cans wouldn't go far.

Grace pulled into the closest spot to the front door she could find. She unhooked the seatbelts and lifted the baby out of the car seat. "Let's go get you some food, little one. Then we can go home and play."

Holly responded with a smile and reached for Grace's necklace.

"No, no, honey." Grace pried it from her fingers and tucked the pendent inside her shirt. She spotted the wet wipes at the entrance and made quick use of them, wiping down the seat and cart handle to eliminate germs, hoping to keep them both healthy.

After scanning the overhead signs, she made her way to the baby section, where she found an entire row of everything imaginable one could need. She was tempted with all the cool gadgets and accessories. Bibs, toys, cups, pacifiers, teething rings... The available choices went on and on.

She shook her head, needing to stay focused. Her budget didn't include nonessentials, especially since her first paycheck in a few months wouldn't come for a couple more weeks. Which was exactly why she couldn't afford to lose the new job.

Grace stopped at the section with powdered milk cans like the one Karen had sent with Holly. It didn't take her long to spot the matching can, and she grabbed one off the shelf, trying to locate the price. *No way*. Even the generic version was cringe-worthy. People complained about the cost of gas and milk, but those items had nothing on baby formula. You'd think it was gold at this price. She grabbed two cans, hoping it would go further than expected.

Next stop, diapers. Another large selection to pick from, but Grace was at a loss when it came to choosing which box. The diapers in her bag didn't exactly come with labels. The sizes meant nothing to her, but then neither did the pounds they listed. "How much do you weigh, baby girl?" Grace laughed as Holly reached out to touch her arm. "What, no answer? Why ever not? Don't blame me if your diapers droop."

A woman approached with a baby similar in size.

"Excuse me, I'm watching Holly—" she pointed to the baby, "—for my cousin, and I need to pick up diapers. I seriously need some help, if you wouldn't mind. There are so many choices and sizes, and I don't have a clue." A woman her age shouldn't be this clueless, but no one she hung out with had a baby except Karen. And even then, Grace didn't see her cousin nearly as often as she would have liked since the baby was born. It had been love at first sight with Holly. Grace and Karen weren't exactly on the same page in life, but when it came to Holly, the pages blurred.

The corners of the woman's mouth lifted ever so slightly as she tried to keep from laughing. "First time around babies? No worries. My daughter is about the same size, and Amanda wears a size three. I think you'll be safe going with this." The woman picked up a box and handed it to Grace. "Trust me on this, don't scrimp on diapers unless you want lots of leakage and wet bedding." She glanced down at the items in Grace's cart.

"And just another small hint, the baby food you picked out is stage one, which is for infants. The food is like soup. She would be eating stage three. The food starts to have soft little chunks to help the babies get used to chewing for the teeth coming in. Right now, they mostly gum it to mush, but they've got a few teeth in there." The kind woman smiled and held up a jar from her cart. "This is what Amanda eats now. They love the peaches, even if it is messy. Just keep plenty of wipes around and good clothes out of reach."

That explained why the carrots in the diaper bag were chunky. It made total sense now. "Thank you ever so much. I need to add wipes to my ever-growing list. I think Holly's mother should have left me with a manual." Grace shook her head and laughed.

"It's a little overwhelming at first, but this is my third child, so it all comes pretty naturally at this point. Good luck to you." The woman certainly had lots of luck she could give away. *Three children. What a blessing.* Grace wouldn't mind the mess if she could have children of her own. But she also knew the woman wasn't referring to her having children.

"Thanks. I have a feeling I'm going to need it." Grace nodded, overwhelmed by how much she didn't know.

The young woman smiled and headed toward the back of the store.

Grace put the jars of food back on the shelf and moved down a few levels in search of stage three. She hadn't even noticed the numbers, just the fact that beans, peas, bananas, rice, and chicken mush in a jar didn't sound appetizing one bit.

She picked up some generic wipes, hoping that was one place she could cut costs. The baby monitors were another story. There were lots of choices, from sound only to video footage, and a wide range of expense to match. Settling on inexpensive, she picked one that would do what she needed—listen for Holly to wake up when she was in another room. The last item on her list was the only nonessential essential—bathtub toys. Just a couple would be nice, especially if it helped keep playtime and water in the tub.

Grace headed for the checkout register, not wanting to find anything else she couldn't live without. The cashier rang up her order, sliding everything across the scanner. Each beep sent the total higher and higher.

"That's $123.58, please," the cashier said, a smile pasted on her face.

"You've got to be kidding?" She knew things added up fast, but this was ridiculous. How did families afford this?

"No, ma'am. Look for yourself." The cashier spun the digital screen around for her inspection. Sure enough, the total was right. At these prices, her bank account would dwindle far faster than she preferred. There wasn't much choice in the matter, so Grace paid the total, but not before putting back the chocolate bar she'd been about to treat herself to after a less-than-stellar first day on the job.

By the time she arrived home, she was exhausted. Another reminder, yet again, of how hard it was to be a single parent, and in some families, even two parents wouldn't make it any easier if someone worked long hours or was away a lot. Parenting was tough.

It gave her a new appreciation for the adoption agency and the decisions they had to make. Grace might not have liked their rejection, but she could see where single parenting, although sometimes a necessity, wasn't always ideal. And they were trying to find excellent homes for the children in their protection.

Maybe, by the time this was over, Grace would learn and adapt enough that she could prove to the agency she was up to the challenge. Maybe then they'd reconsider their decision.

Lucky greeted her at the door, sniffing the air when she spotted the baby. Just when she thought she could kick off her shoes and relax, Grace realized she still needed to take the dog out for a walk. And do it with a baby in tow. It would have to be a short one.

"Hope you get over your fit of jealousy, girl. I promise Holly won't hurt you, and I love you just the same. She dropped the diaper bag by the front door, set the baby down, and made a point of petting Lucky.

The baby stayed close, reaching out a couple of times to touch the dog, look at Grace, and then smile. Lucky sniffed Holly, this time pressing her nose to the side of the baby's face. Lucky licked her cheek, causing Holly to giggle. Nothing like a wet doggy kiss to seal a friendship.

Grace snapped the leash on Lucky, and the three of them headed back outside for a walk around the block. Waving at several neighbors sitting out on their front porch, she didn't bother to stop and chat. There would be too many questions about Holly, and Grace needed some downtime.

Once back home, Grace put the baby in her booster, using the hands-free moment to feed the dog and prepare Holly's dinner. Not that there was much preparation to unscrewing the lid of a jar and warming the contents. She sat down at the kitchen table with Holly, spoon-feeding her with the rubber-tipped spoon she'd found in the diaper bag.

She couldn't resist at least trying the unappetizing orange chunky mush called carrots, and she regretted the decision instantly. Tasteless as far as she was concerned. The baby didn't seem to mind, although most of it ended up on Holly's face and the table, whether by design or accident, Grace didn't know. There was no way to ask Holly and expect a reasonable answer, but the baby did seem content to play in the stuff.

After a quick bath and some playtime, she changed Holly into a cute pink onesie for bedtime. She laid her down in the pack 'n play, hoping she'd fall asleep right away. Grace needed a few minutes of peace and quiet.

Spending a day out of the office with her boss was a little unsettling. She'd struggled with today's outfit, and although her choice had started out perfect, by the time she'd arrived at work, it was more like perfectly ruined. Professional was hardly the image she portrayed now—at this point, she came closer to harried mother and complete wreck. Grace pulled out a pair of jeans and a dressy blouse to lay out for the morning. Better to be prepared and be comfortable. It would be a better suit of armor in dealing with her boss.

Grace set up the baby monitor, relieved to hear Holly babbling, proving the monitor worked. She settled back on the sofa, let out a deep sigh of relief, and flipped on the TV. Her eyes started to drift shut within minutes, exhaustion finally winning over. So much for a relaxing night. Right now, she only wanted a relaxing bed. It had been a long day, and she had to do it all over again tomorrow. At least this time, without the baby in tow.

Provided, of course, her sister showed up. If Faith didn't, Grace could kiss her job goodbye. After setting the alarm extra early, knowing how much time it took to get ready, Grace crawled into bed. She was tempted to call her friend Olivia and tell her about Holly and the job, but it would have to wait until tomorrow. Too tired to even think, she closed her eyes, following Holly into dreamland.

The alarm went off way too early, and Grace rolled over to silence it, not wanting to wake Holly. Lucky raised her head to look at her as if she were crazy, then lowered her head and pretended to ignore her. The dog wasn't ready to start the day and more than likely resented the loss of their regular petting session in the morning.

Grace clambered out of bed and made her way to the bathroom, stopping to grab the monitor. She flipped the power switch on, turned the volume up to the loudest setting, and set it on the back of the toilet where she could listen for the baby if she woke up.

In record time, Grace finished her shower, dried off, and donned the clothes she'd picked out the night before. She made her way to the kitchen, desperate for a cup of coffee. As Grace pressed the start button to brew her favorite hazelnut K-cup,

Holly started to make a few noises. Almost perfect timing.

Grace headed for the bedroom and found Holly standing up and watching the door for her. "Good morning, sunshine." She reached for the baby, who held out her arms with a big smile on her face. It was a smile that could warm anyone's heart and make any day just right. "Let's get you out of that wet diaper and get you dressed for the day. It'll be one less thing Faith will have to do. You need to promise me to be good for her. She's even less experienced than I am." Grace laughed.

Holly grabbed her hair and started to babble—unrecognizable sounds, but the sweetest music. Diapered and dressed, Grace carried Holly to the kitchen, put her in the booster seat, and strapped her in. Lucky had followed them into the kitchen, equally wanting to be fed.

After she put a few of the puffs from the baggy of finger food on the tray, hoping to keep the baby occupied, she turned her focus to fixing Holly's bottle. The baby reached for the bottle eagerly as Grace held it out. She stuck it in her mouth and sucked hard as if she were starved. It was amazing how much milk they could put away.

She fed Lucky and gave her some fresh water. This time, the dog immediately began to eat, a sure sign she was getting used to having Holly around.

Next up, breakfast. Grace mixed up some cereal and then opened a jar of applesauce and poured it into the bowl, mixing the two. She pressed the bowl to the tray, the suction cups keeping it in place. Pulling up a chair, she started to feed the baby, hoping it wouldn't be quite as messy with something that tasted better. The woman's warning at the drugstore last night was good advice, but at least the meal wasn't orange or green this time.

The doorbell rang, and Grace felt as though she were being pulled in six directions, none of them her own. She got up to answer, relieved to see her sister standing in the doorway. "Thanks for coming this time."

"Whatever. Just tell me what I need to do." Faith's surly attitude wasn't welcome, not on a morning that had gone well so far. Her sister reached down to pet Lucky. The dog had come over to sit at Faith's feet, her tail wagging a happy hello.

"It'll be fun, trust me. Just commit yourself to be with Holly, and you'll enjoy it. Forget about everything else. I wish I didn't have to go to work so I could just stay and play with her." Which was precisely why Grace was looking forward to the weekend. It was a shame Karen hadn't needed her when she was still out of work.

"You've always been the settled one. I'm surprised you're not married with three kids of your own by now."

Grace flinched and turned away, not wanting her sister to see the pain she'd caused by her careless words.

"I'm sorry. It just slipped out, and it's not like I don't know. Me and my big mouth." Faith shook her head, the mortified expression on her face proof her sister meant the apology and could discern between right and wrong. Both good qualities to have as she moved into the adult world. It was hard to stay upset with her for something that had been an accidental slip.

"Don't worry about it. As far as the baby's concerned, she needs a bottle every few hours. She'll let you know when she's hungry. Just read the directions on the back of the can. It tells you how much warm water to add. Make sure you test it against your wrist before you give it to her to make sure it's not too hot. For lunch, she gets a jar of baby food, your choice from the not-so-delectable options, and then the same for dinner.

"Her diapers need changing every couple of hours. Stay on top of it; otherwise, you'll be changing her clothes, too. And when she starts to fuss but has had a recent bottle, then it's probably nap time. She has a portable crib in my bedroom, and this is a monitor so you can hear when she wakes up." Grace pointed to the device sitting on the counter.

"Okay. And what do I do with the baby when she's not eating, sleeping, or peeing?" Faith asked jokingly, the first sign her sister was melting.

"You get to play and watch kid movies. Right up your alley. Everything you need is in here—" she held up the diaper bag, "—or on the kitchen counter, or in my top right dresser drawer. Call me on my cell if you need anything at all. I've taped the number of the hospital on the refrigerator, although I hope you won't need anything so drastic as that. And I'll leave you her car seat just in case you need to take her anywhere, but please, only do that if it's an emergency. Otherwise, I'd prefer it if you just stay here."

"Trust me, I have no desire to go anywhere with a baby in tow. Talk about an image killer." Faith grimaced.

Holly pointed at Faith and started laughing, managing to blow bubbles and food in every direction. Luckily, Grace was out of range, and her outfit for the day was safe from a baby baptism.

"Wow. That's gross. I hope you're going to clean it up before you go." Faith looked between her and the baby, shaking her head.

"I could, but there's no sense cleaning her up before she's done eating. You need to finish spoon-feeding her, and Ryan will be here any minute to pick me up." It was more about Grace staying clean for work today, but she didn't need to share that part with her sister.

"Ryan?" Faith looked at her, one eyebrow raised in question.

"My new boss. The one who almost fired me yesterday because I brought a baby to work after my sister bagged out on me for childcare," Grace said, delivering the hit and trying to drive her point home. Her sister needed to learn she wasn't the only one impacted by her decisions.

"I've already apologized, and you still have your job. So lay off, why don't you?"

If her sister wasn't nineteen and quite capable of watching the baby, Grace would have trouble leaving her alone with Holly. But Faith was more bark than bite, something she'd learned years ago. Her little sister was eight years younger than her and resented being the little sister. She'd been treated like a baby until it was too late, and this was the result.

A knock on the door ended their conversation. "I've got to go. I'll call you a couple of times and check in." She leaned down to kiss Holly on the forehead, trying to keep from getting applesauce cereal all over her clothes. Holly reached for her sweater, but Grace managed to evade her outstretched hand. "See you tonight, sweetheart."

"Grace, I really am sorry about what I said. It was an accident. And you don't have to call me and check in. I may not want to be here, but I can take care of the baby. Trust me, I'm not a kid like everyone thinks." Faith had a conscience, her continued effort to apologize was proof of that.

"I know you didn't mean anything by it, and you're forgiven. And just so you know, I wouldn't leave you with the baby if I didn't think you could take care of her, no matter what my situation is. I told you before, have fun with her." Grace smiled, headed for the front door, and pulled it open.

Ryan stood there, two paper cups in his hands. "Good morning. I stopped at the diner and grabbed us coffee for the road. Plus, I wasn't sure you'd be ready, so I thought I'd be prepared to bring them inside while I waited."

"That was nice of you. I think. I mean, automatically assuming I'd be late getting ready is a bit high-handed." Grace took one of the cups from Ryan.

"I only had your history to go by, and odds were on you being late." He chuckled.

"Shows how much you know, because I'm ready to go, smart aleck." She stepped outside and pulled the door closed behind her.

"It's an apology of sorts. I know I was hard on you about the baby. It was an unexpected situation, and nothing I've ever had to deal with before." Ryan slid in the car and reached over to push her door open at the same time she got there.

Grace climbed inside, pulled the door shut, and put on her seat belt, all while juggling her coffee. "Not many of us have had to deal with being vomited and peed on in the same day, especially someone who isn't a parent. I think you handled it rather well." She glanced at him, hoping he'd see the humorous side of the double disaster.

"Let's call it even and start over." The hopeful look on his face made it easy to agree and even easier to forgive him. His warm smile made her want to be friends and get to know him better.

"I'm all for that." Ryan put the car in reverse, and they backed out of the driveway. They drove down Main Street and turned onto the main highway and headed north.

"Nice car," Grace said, checking out the interior of the Mercedes.

"It does its job if that's what you mean," Ryan said, glancing in her direction.

"Any car, well, almost any car can get from point A to point B. This car does it in style. I mean, look at all the controls. Do you even know what half of them do?" Grace reached out to press a couple of buttons on the video screen.

"Surprisingly, no. The car is strictly for image." He shrugged. "When one goes looking for investors, it's best not to arrive in an old beat-up Ford."

"I think there's lots of room between the two."

"True. So maybe I like it. It's got a powerful engine and a smooth ride. Happy?"

"Yes. Honesty is always the best policy." Except in her case, she hadn't exactly been honest with Ryan. Some things were best left alone.

They hadn't gotten very far when Grace suddenly realized she hadn't given Faith the car seat. It was locked in her car and inaccessible. Torn with what to do, she bit her lower lip, trying to gather the courage to ask Ryan to turn around. Her fingers tapped her leg as she tried to reason through the pros and cons.

Just ask. Except they'd just agreed to start over, and this would be like going backward.

"What's wrong? You've grown quiet and tense, and your fingers look like you're tapping out 'The Little Drummer Boy'."

Grace turned to face him. She couldn't possibly let him get as far as Mount Washington ski resort without going back. What if Faith needed the seat and didn't have it? There was just so much to remember when it came to a baby, and clearly, she was terrible at it. "I need to go back to the house. I'm sorry. I forgot to give Faith the car seat. It's locked in my vehicle," Grace added reluctantly.

"Is she planning on taking her anywhere?" Ryan glanced in her direction, slowing down some.

"Not that I know of. But what if something happens, and Faith needs to take the baby to the doctor? Or to the store? Or to my mother's? It's just a precaution. But I can't go this far away and not have a contingency plan in case they need to go somewhere. Like the hospital. What if Holly chokes on something? I won't be able to think straight if I'm worried."

"That's fine. I don't want you to stress over it. It's only five minutes back, and for your peace of mind, it'll be worth it."

"Thank you for being so understanding."

"You can tell this is your first baby." Ryan had absolutely no idea how close he was to the truth. The reality was, it was her first time looking after a baby other than Faith, something she hadn't done in years. And when Faith was Holly's age, their mother had treated her sister like she was a porcelain doll. Which meant Grace hadn't been good enough to be her babysitter until she was almost seven years old. By that time, Grace had been fifteen and not overly excited about having her free time cramped by a kid sister in tow.

They pulled back into the driveway, and Grace slid out of the car and stopped to grab the baby seat. She opened the back door of Faith's car, happy for once her sister didn't feel the need to lock it. Grace buckled the seat in, worried her sister wouldn't get it strapped in correctly. Ten extra seconds for the extra peace of mind. Totally worth it.

Grace headed back to the car and slid in. "Thank you." She pulled out her phone and sent Faith a text to let her know what she'd done.

Ryan backed out of the driveway, and soon they were on their way again, none the worse for wear.

She gazed over at him and admired his strong jaw and clean-cut features. His woodsy cologne drifted her way. *Nice.*

For a woman with a no-date policy, she was way more interested than she wanted to be, especially considering he was her boss. The only explanation that made any sense was his anti-kid status. Half the battle she faced when dating someone new, was already won in his case. An anti-kid guy wouldn't have a problem with a woman who couldn't have children. Unless he changed his mind. And a lot of men did just that.

Maybe she should explain her polycystic condition to Ryan. But then if he rejected her, it would be heartbreaking to know he was rejecting her and not her condition. At least the other guys pretended to like her until they found out she couldn't have kids.

It was going to be a long drive if they had nothing to talk about. And trying not to think of the attractive man sitting next to her as anything other than her boss would be difficult at best. It wasn't fair Ryan was as appealing as a candy cane to a child.

Chapter Six

RYAN HADN'T MINDED GOING back to Grace's place, and he'd tried to make that clear. The truth was, because of her situation, Ryan had built in extra time. Yes, he'd teased her about it, but kids did have a way of messing up the simplest of plans.

"It's about an hour's ride up there. It might be a good chance for us to get to know each other. Seeing as we'll be working together quite closely, it's important."

"What do you want to know?" Grace asked, adjusting her position by turning in his direction slightly.

"Something that's not on your resume, for starters." He grinned, keeping a close eye on the road but also managing to get in a few glances in her direction.

"Fine, but it goes two ways." She took a sip of coffee. "Ask me a question, and I'll answer, and then it's your turn."

Easy enough terms if Grace picked the right questions. "Tell me about Faith." It was a good place to start.

"That's easy. She's my sister, the one who pulled a no-show yesterday. Apparently, my mom set her straight and made her come watch Holly. She graduated from high school last June and has zero ambition to get a job or take responsibility for her life. She's eight years younger than me, and we're not very close. Too big of an age gap for that to happen."

"I'm glad she could help out. I know you say you're not close, but it's probably nice to know she's there." Ryan couldn't help the resentful tone in his voice but hoped Grace hadn't noticed. His own sister had no sense of obligation and had walked out of his life. *A long time ago.*

"I suppose. Do you have any siblings?"

"None that matter." He grimaced. It wasn't a subject he talked about—with anyone. Maybe this get-to-know-you conversation wasn't such a good idea. Either that, or he should have led with a better question.

"What's that supposed to mean?" Grace persisted, not taking his hint.

Ryan pursed his lips and stared ahead at the road, pretending not to have heard her question.

"Come on, your turn to fess up. You agreed to talk." She reached out and touched his arm, forcing him to gaze her way. It was her sweet smile that won him over. Sweet determination. An odd combination.

"I have a sister, but I don't have a clue where she is, and at this point, I don't care. Happy?" Ryan couldn't believe he'd told her that much, as he preferred to keep his private life...well, private.

"Happy? I don't think so. You're going to have to do better than that. You have a sister. Did the two of you fight? Is this one of those age-old battles between siblings that neither one can let go?" She tried to lighten the situation and draw him out, but she didn't know the truth.

The ugly truth. His sister didn't want him.

As a pathetic eight-year-old boy he'd clung to a false hope his big sister would rescue him from the foster care system. It was a hope that faded away with each passing year, until he himself, aged out. "Hardly. I'm not prone to that type of wasted energy."

"What is it then? It can't be that bad. You can't honestly sit here and tell me you don't want to know anything about her. She's family. Somewhere deep down, you must care, whether you're willing to admit it or not."

Ryan glanced her way and shook his head. "Once upon a time, maybe, but that ship sailed a long time ago. In fact, it sunk."

"Why?" Grace pressed him for more, not letting him off the hook.

"Not that it's any of your business, but to stop you from asking more questions, I'll tell you why. When we were kids, we were placed in foster care. She's older than me and the agency moved her to a permanent place. *Without me.* I never heard from her again. End of story.

"I'm sorry. Do you want to tell me what happened?" Grace asked.

It was one thing to have a get-to-know-you conversation, quite another to turn it into a psychoanalysis of the soul. "I'm not looking to unravel or fix anything in your life, and I'd appreciate it if you'd try to do the same for me." He delivered the cutting blow without preamble, effectively stopping the conversation in its tracks.

Grace's look of shock and dismay made him wince. He'd been a jerk to be that rude to her when all she'd wanted to do was help, but it wasn't like he was digging deep into her personal life, like pressing for more information on the baby's father. Some things were better left unsaid, and people were entitled to their secrets.

Grace reached out and touched his arm, shocking him with her gentle touch after he'd been bullish toward her. "I'm sorry. You're right. I won't ask again."

Her words and touch warmed his heart, making him feel worse. But he couldn't break down his walls, especially not with her. Grace Baxter all but shouted relationship, marriage, and family. All words not in his vocabulary. They were a boss and an employee, and anything else was off-limits. "Let's talk about the grand opening and some of the insights I have for the company. It might help give you a better perspective on how to market us."

"That's a great idea. I'd love to hear how you came up with the idea for the company and what you've been through to pull it all together. I sense you've got a lot at stake, and I'm hoping to be a part of the success." Grace smiled, smoothly moving past the previous conversation.

"There is a lot riding on this, and Jordan hired you because he believes you have what it takes to market the company effectively. If he's got faith in you, so do I." For the rest of the ride to the ski resort, they talked about the company, his goals, and his dreams for World Sport Inc., staying on the safe side of conversational subjects.

They pulled into the deserted parking lot of the Mount Washington ski resort. Grace had never visited the place when it wasn't covered in snow and bustling with hundreds of skiers who looked like ants as they took the chairlift to the top of the mountain, only to race back down. Repeatedly.

Growing up, she'd spent some time here with her friends. Images of Tonya and Olivia flittered through her brain, the trio had never been far apart. At least, it had been that way until Tonya's family moved away, and they'd eventually lost contact.

Olivia, of course, was still somewhat local, having moved to Glen Haven with her husband. She'd long since given up her skis in exchange for married life and a family. And with pre-school-age twins and a full-time job, there was no such thing as free time for her. Something Grace was beginning to understand more, even though she'd only been at this parenting thing for two days. It was the same reason Grace hadn't reached out to her for help with Holly and wouldn't if she could avoid it. Her friend had more than enough going on.

A tall man with a full beard came out of the building and headed in their direction. His rugged mountain-man appearance was a bit gruff for her taste, but some people really went for the woodsy type.

"It's good to see you again, Ryan." The two men shook hands.

"Likewise. Charles, this is Grace, my administrative assistant, and our marketing guru. She's the one Jordan picked to help make this entire endeavor a success."

"Nice to meet you." He reached out, his large rough-skinned hand grasping hers in a firm handshake.

"It's a pleasure to meet you, Charles. I've skied here many times and love this place. It's beautiful this time of year. All the azaleas, roses, and other flowering plants bursting with color are a wonderful change to the massive amounts of white snow I usually see." She glanced around, admiring the peacefulness this time of year.

"It is nice here in the summer. That's why I'm hoping to bring in more foot traffic with other activities and, of course, the World Sport connection. But don't let Ryan load you with too much pressure. I've known this guy for a long time. He wouldn't have invested heavily in this venture if he didn't think it would fly. Don't be afraid to push back when he grumbles. He's a softie at heart." Charles had a sense of humor and came bearing good advice Grace would do well to remember.

"Maybe we could get a coffee sometime, and you can fill me in with more deets," Grace said, trying to rile Ryan a bit.

"Can't a man have any secrets?" Ryan shook his head, clearly not happy with being the subject of discussion.

Grace laughed at his sour expression. "It's not anything I haven't already figured out." *Or suspected.*

Ryan's brow shot up, and his questioning gaze settled on her.

"I'd love to take you to lunch sometime," Charles said, sending a wink in her direction.

Ryan's scowl deepened. "I hardly think that's necessary." Did he hate the idea of people talking about him behind his back? Or was this more about her going to lunch with his friend?

"He's the boss." She jerked her thumb in Ryan's direction, not willing to push him to find out. Besides, her current household situation precluded going on dates anyway.

"Shall we go inside and check on everything?" Ryan asked, satisfied with her answer judging by the look he shot her. She'd have to ask him later what he had against her going out with Charles. He was a friend, after all.

"Sounds good. All the inventory arrived yesterday, and I had my guys working through the night to set it up as per your instructions. They got most of it out already, enough for you to get a good feel for the layout. Did you bring the signage?" Charles glanced at Ryan as they passed through the front door into the shop.

"I did." He tapped his briefcase. "Got it all here."

"What made you pick this area for the start-up of your company?" Grace asked.

"Being a city kid, I always dreamed about the country." He shrugged, as though not wanting to get into the subject.

"Come on, something directed you this way. It's important for me to understand what makes you tick." He glanced at her ruefully and shook his head. "If you say so. Maybe I simply wanted out of the city, and it was as good a place as any to settle down for a bit before I move to open the next location."

"So, you're the jet-setter that will open the new stores?" That didn't sound very settled to her. More like someone with wanderlust. The question was, where did it come from?

"I am. Charles and I go back a way, and his place was as good as any to start. This place is crawling with people in the winter, and like he said, he wants to turn it into a summer destination as well. It works with what we need and expect from our limited store locations."

"What he's not telling you is that he came here during a couple of college winter breaks with me, and he fell in love with Mount Washington National Forest. This guy is as outdoorsy as it gets for a city slicker." Charles laughed, clapping Ryan on the back.

Outdoorsy was not something she'd picked up on considering his tailored suits and fancy car.

"There is that." Ryan nodded.

"Well, I think it's an excellent idea and choice. It's an incredible venture, well-thought-out, and extremely strategic. I'm looking forward to the grand opening next week and seeing how this plays out in the months to come. I can't see it turning out as anything other than a success. Specializing in a small piece of the online retail market is genius.

There's only so much the big players can handle without losing the needed support and tech help that comes with the products."

"I'm glad you approve," Ryan said dryly. Considering the success will largely affect your paycheck."

"There is that," she teased, mocking Ryan's earlier comment.

Charles chuckled. "She sounded like a walking advertising agency trying to drum up investors or sales." He shot her a wink, letting her know he was teasing. Had he also picked up on the idea Ryan didn't seem to like him chummy with her? And if so, why?

"Ha-ha. It's not a canned pitch. It's the truth. And the truth comes easily," Grace added. "Where's the next location?"

"I don't have any...yet. I need to do more research than picking a friend's place that happens to be close to the warehouse. The next one needs to be based on customer and sales concentrations. We won't open but a handful more for brand recognition and ease of possible added shipping centers."

"Then pick a resort destination and send me to do the research." She grinned.

"You'd like that. I think you've got your hands full as it is. I'll figure something out in due time." Ryan smiled, turning to inspect the ski shop.

Grace remembered the place well and was impressed with the changes made to the place. Now doubled in size, the cafeteria bar had been pushed to a new wing addition, a beautiful glass wall allowing people to eat and drink to their heart's content, all while staying warm inside and watching the action on the slopes. The huge fireplace in a corner furnished with several sofa groupings would also be a drawcard. The relaxed atmosphere begged a person to stop and chat over a drink, or perhaps read a book. And of course, plenty of time to shop.

"I love this. You've done an amazing job. I haven't been here in a couple of years, but this is incredible."

"Thanks, but I can't take credit for the idea. That all goes back to this guy." He nodded toward Ryan. "He's the visionary."

"Wow. I'm impressed." Grace smiled at Ryan, meaning every word.

"Thanks. I'm motivated by the investors I answer to." He brushed off her compliment as though he were uncomfortable with any focus or accolades thrown his way. It made her wonder more about his past and what had soured him on any chance of family and happiness. The man had a kind heart, and it would be wasted if all it ever focused on was the next business deal.

"Don't let him fool you. He's always been a genius when it comes to this stuff. That's what happens when you keep your head buried in the books all the time instead of partying with the rest of us normal college pukes." Charles chuckled, shaking his head as if studying had been a waste of time when there were more important things to do like having fun. Good thing the guy opened a place designed to provide non-stop entertainment. And hopefully not just for the winter season anymore.

"What can I say? Work motivates me."

"Much to the dismay of half the female college population," Charles chortled.

"I think you took care of my fair share." Ryan grinned and shook his head. "Enough about my private life."

Grace wondered why an attractive, smart man, with apparently no shortage of women offering to partner with him, wouldn't have already been caught by the matrimonial ring. Was it one more thing that came back to the sister he wouldn't talk about? And if so, when would Ryan let go of the past and be able to embrace a happy future? Something she knew without a doubt he deserved.

"The place looks great, Charles. Here are the signs." Ryan handed them each a stack. "Maybe we can start matching these up and hanging them in front of the products where they belong," he suggested.

Grace shuffled through the ones he'd given her. They were boring, standard price-point signs. A description followed by a small starburst with a price inside—something every computer program had—including the free ones. Nothing eye-catching or creative or unique about them at all. She glanced around the place, trying to picture it on opening day. Everyone would be searching for the next big grand-opening special they couldn't live without.

"I have a suggestion," Grace spoke up, not blown away by what she was seeing.

The two men stopped hanging signs to look up at her.

"What's that? You're the marketing genius, and we bow down to you," Ryan teased, crossing the room to join her.

"I'll have to remember that in the future." She laughed. "I think these signs are too monotonous. Sorry," she added, trying to take the sting off her comment.

Ryan grimaced, taking a deep breath, but remained silent.

"I'm not saying whoever did this did a bad job. It's just not a great job. I think it can be better." They were terrible, but it wouldn't do any good to point out the obvious, especially if it turned out Ryan made them. She'd learned early on that constructive criticism yielded far better results than open dislike.

"What do you suggest?" Charles asked, clearly trying to temper the situation.

"I think they need more color and more snap. The description doesn't have to be on the card, just the item name. All this extra verbiage can go away, leaving room for bigger, more attention-getting designs with offsetting colors to attract the eye." It wasn't a big switch, but the results could be fantastic. Price signs the same size and design had proved to be a failure when it came to attracting a customer to stop and look.

"There's no time to do that at this point," Ryan said, dismissing her suggestion.

"What if I get it done and bring them back by Monday morning first thing?" It was a crazy offer, given that she had to deal with Holly, but she couldn't let this opportunity to make things right pass by. Besides, it would go a long way to making amends with Ryan considering her first-day disasters.

"Did you forget we've got Spring Fling Saturday?"

"Spring Fling?" She knew the festival was Saturday in Lancaster, but not what it had to do with her.

"I emailed you about it. We have a booth, and you're expected to help by talking to people about the company and sharing our vision. Please tell me you saw the email?" He frowned.

"I must have missed that one somehow. I was planning on taking Holly to the festival." This put a kink in her plans. Especially if she continued to insist on remaking the signs. She'd make it all work. Somehow.

"You'll have lots of free weekends with your daughter, but Spring Fling is only one day a year, and the kick-off to our grand opening Monday. That only happens once."

Not true, but Ryan didn't know that. "Fine. But be forewarned, I'm bringing Holly. It is technically my day off." She grinned. "And I'll still take care of the signs. The printer can handle the order, and I'll personally deliver them."

"Forewarning duly noted. And as to the signs, if you're up to it, who am I to say no? What should we do with these?" Ryan asked, holding some of the signs up.

"Throw them in the trash. No offense." So much for diplomacy, but Grace was determined for him to agree.

"None taken. It's not like I spent a ton of time designing them, as you can tell." *Ouch.*

"You did these? I'm sorry." Her face grew heated, realizing she'd put her big size nine foot in her mouth.

"Don't worry about it. If you want to replace the signs, knock yourself out. Just make the ads and flyers your priority. Those are the real outreach to a potential customer base that can make or break this launch." Ryan locked gazes with her, his expression unreadable.

"I'm already halfway through revamping the first set of ads. Relax."

They spent the next few hours putting out the rest of the inventory since they didn't have to work on the signage. Grace used the time to rearrange some of the racks and displays, focusing on color splashes and groupings. The project had become way more involved than they'd originally planned, but with the efforts of the two men, they managed to get through it. Neither one of them questioned her when she asked to move some displays repeatedly, they just did as she asked and bit back any response.

Grace stepped back to look at the overall effect, pleased with what she saw. "This is so much better. Don't you agree?"

The two men came to stand next to her.

"It is, there's no doubt about it. I'm glad I brought you along today and that we had no distractions," Ryan said, his well-meaning words a clear message.

There might not have been a baby distraction, but to say there'd been no distractions wasn't even close to the truth. She'd spent the afternoon watching Ryan at work and bumping shoulders with him on occasion. It was a distraction she couldn't afford, but one that was hard to ignore. There was something about him that drew her close, and clearly, based on the number of times she caught him gazing at her with an odd expression on his face, he was finding it hard to ignore as well.

Chapter Seven

♥

IT HAD BEEN AN interesting day, one that left Ryan with mixed emotions. Working side-by-side with Grace in such a relaxed environment, he couldn't stop himself from watching her. Her light laughter, her creative touches, her insights, all proof of the amazing woman she was. Entirely unlike the scatterbrained mother he'd met at the bakery and at the office yesterday. Two completely different people.

He respected and admired her talents, but a part of him couldn't help but acknowledge that down-home fresh and wholesomeness that kept calling him. The love she gave her daughter and exuded in her daily life, even during rough times, was something he found himself drawn toward. In the past, trouble only meant run. What was it about her that drew him like a moth to a flame?

They drove back to Hallbrook, most of the conversation centered on the ski shop and the grand opening. They were both clearly avoiding personal conversation. The issues that had arisen earlier this morning were still very much in the forefront and standing like a wall between them.

"Are you all set tomorrow with your sister to babysit?" It was a stretch, but he was trying to ease the awkward silence that had fallen in the car.

"Yes. Faith got the lecture about honoring commitments and responsibility. Trust me, it's a lesson my sister needs to learn."

"Wasn't your sister watching Holly before you came to work for me?" He turned to look at her, a little perplexed by her sister's change of heart.

"No. I wasn't working. Before that, Holly had other care when it was needed." Grace shrugged.

"Why isn't Faith going to college? Does she have any idea what she wants to do with her life?"

She looked at him and shook her head. "Nope. She says she's tired of school. Tired of doing things she doesn't want to do. She thinks it's time to have fun. I think it's an affliction of the next generation because my younger cousin has the same problem."

"That's not good. What interests and hobbies does your sister have? Maybe it's a question of pointing her in the right direction." He was grasping at straws, trying to come up with some proverbial words of wisdom.

"Trust me, I've tried to help her find that direction," Grace said, shaking her head. The tone of her indicated he'd hit a sensitive nerve.

"I didn't mean to offend you. It's just that maybe since the last time you two talked, your sister is more ready to listen. Life has a way of changing one's perspective." So much for not getting overly personal in their conversation.

"Spoken from a guy who won't talk about his sister, and it's been what, ten or fifteen years, and you're still not talking."

Ouch. Unfortunately, Grace was right. "Twenty-two years to be exact. And, yes, some things don't need talking about."

"Well, hopefully, it doesn't take my sister twenty-two years to figure her life out." Her barb was like a sucker punch to the gut.

"Now that, is something we can agree on," Ryan said, adding a certain finality to his voice and hoping Grace would take the hint.

"Tell me about your sister, please. It's clearly bothering you, and maybe all you need is to just talk about it. Were you two close before you were separated?" Her voice was soft and sweet, compelling him to confide in her.

"No." Maybe telling Grace would put an end to her interest. The fact he was even considering sharing with her should have been a warning sign of major proportions. But what if she was right, and he'd been holding on too tightly?

"I told you we were in a foster home. I used to imagine I never heard from her because her family wouldn't let her get in touch with me. After she would have turned eighteen and I still didn't hear anything, I finally had to accept she didn't want to see me. Her silence was by choice. I stopped giving her the power to hurt me and I let go. As far as I'm concerned, I no longer have a sister." He shrugged, trying to push past the pain talking about the past had brought to the surface.

Grace had a way of getting him to break his silence, but there wasn't anything she could do to fix the issue. The past was broken like a china vase smashed into hundreds of pieces.

"You may think it stopped hurting you, but your answers say something different. Maybe there's a reason or information you don't know, and your wrong. Why not give her a chance to explain? Maybe she's just as afraid of reaching out to you, as you are to her?"

Ryan didn't want Grace to be right. She wasn't telling him anything he hadn't thought to himself over the years. "Who said I'm afraid to reach out to her?"

"Are you?" Grace's question was direct and to the point, the intensity of her gaze burning into the side of his head.

"No. I choose not to, there's a difference." And he had the choice, his sister had seen to that. *Finally.*

"Have you even tried to locate her?" Grace persisted.

"I don't need to. I know how to get in touch with Bella," Ryan said, shrugging his shoulders. *Knowing didn't change a thing.*

Grace reached out and touched his arm. Something she seemed to make a habit of considering this was the third time today. *Yes, he was counting*.

"You do?" she asked, her voice low and urgent. "Since when?"

"Yes. For the past twelve months, I've been getting an email forwarded through the foster care agency. Bella's been trying to find me and wants to talk. I think the time for conversation has long gone. No reason to dredge up the past." Saying it out loud didn't sound nearly as convincing as it did in his head.

"Maybe she regrets what she did and is trying to make amends. Maybe she had no control over the situation. How could you not want to talk to her, even if it's just for closure? You say it's in the past, and it's not bothering you, but clearly, it is. Your actions speak louder than your words."

He glanced down at her hand that had a firm grip on his arm, demanding his attention. "When did you get a psychology degree?"

"I don't need a degree to see the hurt and the pain in your face. And it doesn't take an expert to tell someone to face their issues head on. One way or the other, you both deserve closure."

"I can't. It's a nice thought. But I don't have a sister, so there's no one I need to talk to." Grace didn't understand the years of longing while he'd waited for Bella. The pain of losing his parents and his sister and being all alone, and never really fitting in. A conversation couldn't ease the heartache and hurt and loneliness he'd experienced as a young boy. Nothing could. Ryan had spent his life focused on his career, financial stability, and avoiding relationships and family at all cost. It was a matter of self-preservation and something she would never understand.

"Ryan—"

"Let it go, Grace." The sight of her driveway was a welcome one, signaling the end of the conversation. He pulled into the driveway and shut off the car. "I appreciate what you're trying to do. There's just so much anger and hurt. It's not easy to shove it all aside and open the wounds you spent years closing."

"Okay. I'm sorry. Would you like to come inside? I can offer you a glass of wine or coffee, and I promise no more personal conversation. It's been a good day, and maybe it would be nice for you to meet Holly on her own home turf. And you can tell me why you don't think I should go out with your friend." Grace grinned, her efforts to ease them past the awkward moment sweet and much appreciated.

Ryan was tempted. At least he had been until she mentioned the baby. "Thanks for the offer, but it's probably not a good idea. We've got a big day tomorrow at the office, and I've got a lot to do in preparation. As for Charles, he's a lady's man. Not the settling-down type, and with Holly, not exactly the kind of guy you need in your life. Just my two cents." He shrugged.

He hated the look of disappointment on Grace's face, but it couldn't be helped. Going in for a glass of wine would be personal of a different kind. He was all too aware of the mutual attraction they felt, but that's where it had to stop. He was her boss, and it was a line he wouldn't cross.

Grace had offered Faith her second bedroom when she'd arrived home last night, thinking it might be easier if she stayed at the house during the week.

Her sister had declined and left quickly, a date with her friends in town calling her name. Faith hadn't said much about her day with Holly, other than that there had been no problems. Cut and dried and nothing short of what Grace had expected. There hadn't been any desperate calls throughout the day for help, and Grace had shown restraint in not checking up on Holly, for no other reason than to prove to Faith she trusted her.

What Grace hadn't expected, though, was Faith's heartfelt goodbye to the baby, consisting of a hug and kiss to the top of her head, with a promise to see her tomorrow. Her sister might not want to admit it, but she clearly enjoyed spending time with Holly. But then who wouldn't? Aside from Karen, that is. Grace shook her head. It was unthinkable Karen hadn't bothered to even call and check on her daughter.

Speaking of calling people, Grace still hadn't phoned Olivia to tell her what was going on. And right about now, she could use her friend's emotional support and unerring wisdom. She hit the speed dial for Olivia and waited for her friend to answer.

"Hey, Grace. I haven't heard from you in days."

"I know how busy you are, and things have been pretty hectic on my end as well. Do you have time to catch up, or should we try another night?"

"Now is perfect. Danny's out in the backyard with the twins, and I'm fixing dinner. I'll put you on speakerphone. I want to hear all about your new job."

"So, what's new with you?" Grace asked, hoping to ease into the reason for her call.

"Don't even try that with me. You know my excitement is centered around four-year-old boys and the day-to-day excitement about who said what, to who, or who has whose stuff. You know the routine." Olivia laughed.

"I do." Grace did know, having experienced it firsthand when visiting her friend.

"Start talking. I want updates." Olivia would have to settle for a modified version.

"How about I give you the speed dial version of my life? It may be all the time I have," Grace said, glancing at the baby happily playing on her blanket. *For the moment.*

"What's that supposed to mean?"

"You'll understand in a minute. So, about the job. As far as a first day goes, mine was a disaster. There were a few hiccups along the way."

"Hiccups?" Olivia asked.

"Well, more like vomiting," Grace said, wincing as she recalled Ryan covered in baby puke. She filled Olivia in about Holly, her job, and Ryan, trying to gloss over the extra details and sticking to the core facts, knowing at any minute, either one of them could be called to duty elsewhere.

"I can't believe you didn't call me sooner," her friend exclaimed. "I should have said no to Karen, but I couldn't. You get it, don't you? I'm mean you know my situation and all."

"Sometimes, you go too far with your kindness. Spreading yourself too thin. But Grace, I do understand. Honestly. The good news is you still have your job, and Faith is helping you now. I'm looking for the silver lining in this mess you've landed in with your generosity. Is there anything I can do to help?" It was sweet of Olivia to offer, but Grace knew better than to take advantage of her friend.

"No, but thanks. With Faith back on track, I swear I'm good. And Ryan and I have an understanding." *Mostly, anyway.*

"Sounds to me like you're interested in the guy?"

Olivia was right, but Grace wasn't ready to get into that aspect of things. "Hardly. Ryan's my boss. The only thing I like is that he didn't fire me. And of course, he's good with Holly."

"What?" Olivia exclaimed.

"He sort of helped out at the office with her. It's no big deal, really," Grace said, trying to prove it to herself as much as convince Olivia.

"No big deal? You're crazy." A flurry of activity could be heard in the background. "Tell her, Danny. If a guy steps in and helps you take care of your baby and he's not the father, it's a big deal. Like, he's interested. Right?"

"Who are you talking to?" Danny asked, completely blindsided and clearly confused by Olivia's question.

"Grace, of course," her friend answered, as if the answer should have been obvious.

"But she doesn't have a baby." The poor guy had no clue what he'd walked into.

"She does now. It's a long story. But it's a big deal, right?" Olivia persisted.

"Based on what you've said, it is, but it's not like I know all the facts." Spoken like a true male. Cover the bases on both sides to make sure you didn't come up the loser.

"You know enough." Olivia laughed. "See, Grace. It *is* a big deal."

"I can't believe you just dragged Danny into this. Ryan and I have a working relationship. Besides, I've already started off with a lie, so it's kind of hard to expect anything good to come of it."

"What lie? You didn't say anything about lying to the man," Olivia said, picking up on Grace's comment.

"He thinks Holly is mine." She waited for Olivia to read her the riot act.

"You're insane. Why would you tell him that?"

"To keep my job. If he found out I was only babysitting, he would have fired me for bringing her. Ryan also assumes I'm husband hunting, so I think it's safe to say he isn't interested, especially when you consider his anti-kid, anti-relationship status."

"And how would you know about that?"

"We talked, and it came up." Grace had shared more than enough information for one day. If she told her about Charles' invitation and Ryan's reaction, it would be tantamount to sealing her friend's already-formed opinion.

The sound of children yelling in the background grew louder. "Listen, duty calls, and I've got to run. You need to keep me posted and let me know if there's anything I can do to help. My advice is to set the record straight with Ryan. No good comes from lies, and you know it. And we need to finish this chat soon."

"Go. It's all good. I promise. I just thought you should know what was going on, so you didn't feel left out." Grace laughed.

"I do anyway." It sounded like glass breaking in the background. "Got to go while I have any dishes left." Olivia was gone before she could respond.

As hectic as it sounded at her friend's house, she still envied her the family life she enjoyed. Grace knew it wasn't all chaos.

Chapter Eight

♥

THE ALARM WENT OFF, and Grace rolled over, stretching to turn off the offensive sound before it woke the baby. Holly was still peacefully asleep in her portable crib, allowing Grace to get ready for work without any trouble. Lucky ran after her into the kitchen, happy to get some attention as Grace reached down and petted the dog. A few good scratches later, and she happily ran off, back to the bedroom to play protector.

It wasn't long before Holly could be heard moving about and talking to Lucky. *More like babbling.*

She went into the bedroom, eager to share a few special moments with Holly before having to leave for work. "Good morning, sunshine," she said, picking the baby up and moving her to the bed to smother her with kisses. After getting the baby dressed, Grace took a few minutes to put Holly's stuff in one location, trying to make things easier on her sister.

In the kitchen, she set the baby in her highchair, before mixing up a bowl of cereal. Grace sat next to Holly and spoon-fed her, impressed by how fast the baby ate. She was equally impressed there wasn't a single drop of food on her work clothes. Grace was becoming an old pro at this baby business, or so it seemed.

Lucky, on the other hand, wasn't happy about it. She'd learned quickly to stick around for unexpected treats that fell to the floor and was disappointed when there weren't any this time around.

Grace fixed Holly a bottle and handed it to her. Glancing at her watch, she was surprised Faith hadn't arrived yet. She shoved the papers she'd been working on last night into her briefcase, closed the latches, and set it by the door so she'd be ready to go.

Come on, Faith. Where are you? Grace glanced out the front window and peered down the street. A wave of dread filled her, causing her stomach to clench. There was no way her sister would do this to her again. *No way.*

Her phone rang, Faith's ringtone booming like a death knoll in the midst of the room, a foreboding shadow of what was to come. There was only one reason her sister would be calling at this moment. Grace snatched up the phone. "Where are you? You should have been here ten minutes ago."

"I'm having car trouble, and I can't make it. I'm sorry." Car trouble was one of the oldest excuses in the book. In Faith's language, it meant *I stayed out late partying*. Sorry wouldn't fix the mess.

"Really? I can't believe you'd do this to me again. You're so irresponsible. When are you going to grow up and take responsibility for your actions?" Grace tried to collect her thoughts, shaking her head as she glanced back at the baby.

"It's not my fault, and I can't very well walk there, now can I?" Her sister's sarcasm did little to calm Grace down.

"Not your fault? Nothing is ever your fault, is it? Never mind. I'm late enough as it is. Sleep in, play with your friends, do whatever. I'm done." Grace hung up the phone, more furious with her sister than she'd been in a long time. Enough was enough. Faith was their mother's problem, and the two of them could hash this one out.

Olivia had offered her help, but there was no way she'd call her friend. She had enough on her plate without Grace adding to the mix. Left with no choice, she was forced to take the baby to work. *Again.*

The rash decision to take care of Holly was ruining her life, but somehow, she'd find a way to deal with the consequences. Because there was one thing Grace was certain of, she'd say yes all over again in a New York second. The chance to love and care for a baby had been an answer to her prayers, and it was with prayer she'd see this through.

Grace took a deep breath and exhaled, gathering her thoughts. After loading the diaper bag with every possible contingency, she changed Holly's diaper and then dressed her in a sweater to ward off the morning chill. She grabbed the diaper bag, her handbag, the car seat, and the baby, and headed out the door.

It was like packing for a month's vacation every time you took a baby anywhere. Setting Holly down in the back seat, Grace hooked up the straps that held the baby seat in place. She needed six hands to manage the buckles and keep Holly from playing with every button she found.

"Here you go, sweetheart. Time to get in your car seat." The answering babble of sounds made Grace stop and smile.

Driving a little over the speed limit, she tried to make up time, not wanting to be late. She was also hoping to sneak into her office and keep Holly off Ryan's radar. Otherwise, yesterday's truce would end.

Grace glanced around the parking lot for Ryan's car as she pulled in. She let out a huge sigh of relief when it was nowhere to be seen. Gathering up everything she needed, Grace made her way to her office and closed the door behind her. She spread out the blanket in the corner with some toys, much the same way she'd done the first day. "Be a good girl, honey. Please." Grace gave her a kiss on the head and moved to sit down at her desk, firing up the computer.

She'd worked out several ideas for the price signage last night, and she was eager to put the order in. The printer had agreed to handle the fast turn-around, but only if she turned in the mockups by five p.m. today. She could pick them up on Friday and deliver them on Saturday. And as to the extra expense, that was Ryan's problem. Hers was just to make sure it happened.

Stopping only to change the baby's diaper, give her some snacks, and fix two bottles, Grace was pleased with the amount of work she accomplished throughout the morning. She'd even slipped in a few minutes to play with the baby, something she couldn't resist.

Holly had been asleep for the past ninety minutes, making it even easier to concentrate. And there was still no sign of Ryan. Everything was going perfect.

Five minutes later, perfect ended; Holly waking up and screaming at the top of her lungs. Grace rushed to her side and picked her up. She touched the baby's forehead with the back of her hand, relieved Holly wasn't burning up with a fever. Crocodile tears rolled down the baby's face, breaking Grace's heart as she tried to comfort her, unsure what was wrong or how to fix it.

"*Shhh*. There, now. It'll be all right." Grace changed Holly's diaper, hoping the obvious solution would be the right one. Except the cries continued. She tried toys to entertain and bouncing the baby on her hip while she paced the room, but nothing helped.

The door burst open, and Grace looked up to discover Ryan standing there, a deep frown etched on his face.

Busted.

"I can explain."

"No explanation needed. The baby is back, and apparently not happy. It doesn't matter why she's here, just that she is." There was some truth to what he said, and Ryan would no more buy into Faith's lame excuse than she had. But Grace felt the need to explain anyway.

"It's Faith. I told you about her yesterday. She's so irresponsible. I should have known better than to think I could trust her. I'm sorry."

"What's wrong with Holly?" He nodded toward the baby, ignoring everything she'd said about Faith.

"I don't know. She woke up from her nap and started screaming. Maybe she had a bad dream." Grace remembered the paci in the diaper bag and searched for it frantically, hoping it would do the trick. She stuck it in Holly's mouth and waited. Within seconds, the crying subsided, a good sign she was on the right track.

"I may regret this, but is there anything I can do to help?" Ryan's offer shocked her to the core. So much so, her initial inclination was to refuse, but then she thought better of it.

She could use his help and he was offering. "Really? You'd do that?" Her gaze landed on him, as she tried to decide what to do. He was dressed in a clean shirt, tie, and suit. Grace couldn't handle too many dry-cleaning bills.

"If it will help stop the crying, I'm game." He shrugged.

"Could you hold her?" It was the same thing she'd asked him last time, right before Holly vomited all over him, but she couldn't resist the urge to push Ryan's buttons.

"Really? Last time I did that, it was a disaster. Both times, actually."

"She's dry, I just changed her. She hasn't had any milk in a couple of hours. I think you're safe. I need to fix her bottle. It would be easier for you to hold her and me to fix it, than for me to give you instructions while she's crying." Grace held the baby out to him, assuming he would comply.

"Fine," he said, taking her. Holly's cries subsided almost instantly as she checked Ryan out, curious about the new person holding her.

Grace hadn't even made it to the door with the formula yet, and she stopped to look back, checking to make sure everything was okay. "What did you do?"

Ryan grinned. "I'm a baby whisperer of sorts. Didn't anyone tell you?"

Grace rolled her eyes. "Baby whisperers don't get vomited and peed on, wise guy."

"True." He nodded. "Honestly, I didn't do a thing. She seems fascinated with my tie."

Grace wasn't about to take any chances and dally, pressing the good fortune of silence. "Maybe she likes bright colors. Don't move, I'll be right back with a bottle, just in case she starts crying again." She hurried down the hall, anxious to get back. So much for keeping the baby a secret. Ryan hadn't been happy about the situation, but at least he hadn't fired her on the spot. But by now, Grace was starting to notice a pattern. Ryan Walker was one of the good guys, whether he liked it or not.

And the image of him holding the baby was one that would be imprinted on her heart forever. The man took to Holly like a natural, and vice versa. And there was something else Grace couldn't help but notice. Holly looked like Ryan with her dark hair and olive skin complexion, so much so, they could easily pass for father and daughter

Ryan was loath to admit it, but the minute Holly stopped crying and looked up at him with her big, blue, tear-filled eyes, his heart melted like ice on a sunny day. Who could resist adorable?

It had only taken seconds for him to identify the sound of a baby crying when he came in from the plant. And just as quickly, he'd zeroed in on the source. He'd meant what he said to Grace, it didn't matter why Holly was here, only that she was. Babies didn't belong at work, and at some point, Grace would need to work out her childcare issues.

For now, nothing else had changed. He still needed Grace for her office skills and her marketing expertise, which meant he'd have to do what he could to make sure she had time to get her job done. And that included helping with Holly.

How hard could it be? She was just a baby and not even walking yet. And as a bonus, she liked him. Apparently, he had a way with babies, which was surprising considering his lack of experience in the area.

He grinned at Holly. "You like my tie, don't you? It's not the first one you've obliterated, so have at it. They can be replaced, your mommy can't." Holly tried to stick her finger in his mouth. He twisted his face away, unwilling to go that far, thinking of all the germs.

Grace returned within minutes and handed the bottle to Holly.

"Do I need to hold it or something? Or is she old enough to do this on her own?" Ryan asked.

"See for yourself."

He glanced down and watched as Holly made quick work of the bottle, her two hands wrapped tightly around the plastic to hold it in place.

"I can take it from here. If you put Holly on the blanket, she'll finish her bottle and then play. Thanks for helping me out. I'm sure she'll be just fine now." Grace moved an extra blanket to make a wedge.

"Not a problem. The minute I heard her crying, I decided it was better to help you rather than to get all cranked up about it. It is just temporary, right?" It was the truth, but he also wasn't looking to set a precedent. He needed to be clear on office expectations, even if they'd been overruled since the day he'd met Grace.

"Absolutely. Thank you for working with me on this." Grace's smile warmed his heart as much as Holly's had done moments ago. They were smiles a man could get used to and sharing on a regular basis.

It came as a shock to realize exactly where his thoughts had wandered—a place he'd never let himself go before. Thinking of home and women in the same thought was like the unspoken language for a relationship. "No problem." Ryan went down on one knee, gently laying Holly down against the wedge.

The baby immediately thrust her bottle to the side and started crying. Her lower lip trembled as tears began to fall. Ryan picked her back up, and she quit crying. He turned to Grace and frowned. "Now what do I do?"

"If you've got a couple of hours, you can sit on the floor with her." Grace shook her head and laughed. "Apparently, she's quite smitten with you."

Ryan couldn't find it in his heart to be upset. In fact, he found Holly's adoration satisfying. No one would believe him if he told them. "Yeah, well, that won't help the agony of sitting on the floor for a few hours. I'll pass." Ryan let out a deep sigh, trying to mentally review options. "Do you need to take the afternoon off?"

"That's a sweet offer and way more than I deserve. But I can't afford to leave. I need to finish the sign mockups and get them to the printshop by five. I'll figure something out. Maybe she will settle down once you're out of sight. You know the adage, out of sight—out of mind."

Ryan preferred to think it wouldn't be that easy for either one of them, not that he'd tell Grace that. Some things were best kept private. "What if I take her on a tour of the building and give you some dedicated time to work? A compromise of sorts. I mean, with her mommy just around the corner, how hard can it be?"

"I'm not..." Grace stopped midsentence and looked away, fiddling with the diaper bag. It was clear she didn't trust him to care for her daughter, and the truth stung a little. Or a lot.

"It was just an idea. Sorry." He started to hand Holly over to Grace, hoping to extricate himself from the situation altogether.

"No. It's not that. I don't mind if you're sure. It just doesn't seem very professional."

"I'm thinking a baby in a warehouse is already way past professional. What's one step further? At least I can still talk to the other employees and take care of some business. Boss's prerogative." Ryan winked at Grace, unable to resist teasing her.

Grace smiled, stepping in close to wrap them both in an excited hug. "Thank you."

With a thank-you like that, he'd have to find ways to make her happy more often. For the brief second she'd been in his arms, Ryan liked it. A lot. The scent of jasmine swirled around him, tingling his senses long after she'd pulled back.

Ryan left her office before he made the mistake of saying anything, not wanting to make the situation between them more confusing than it already was. He toted Holly around the warehouse, pointing out things as they went. The big, noisy equipment toting boxes around. Shelf after shelf of product. The loading dock. And of course, the employees, whose shocked expressions made him laugh. It was totally out of character, and yet it didn't bother him one iota. Not even with the grand opening next week.

The investors might view the situation differently, but they weren't here. Holly was adorable and was quickly wrapping herself around his heart and squeezing. He kept the baby entertained, only stopping by Grace's office occasionally and only for a few minutes at a time to let her know Holly was okay. Well, that, and to let Grace change the baby's diaper.

By the end of the day, Holly was his new best friend, not to mention his youngest. Something he couldn't let Grace find out. He wasn't in the market for a relationship or an instafamily, something he could well imagine Grace would want at this point in her life. It wouldn't do to give her the wrong impression and lead her to think this was anything more than it was—a boss temporarily helping to keep a valuable employee. *Temporarily,* of course, being the operative word.

Ryan dropped Holly off at Grace's office when it was time for him to leave. "Hope you got a lot done today. I don't plan to make a habit of babysitting. It's not my thing. Besides, it ruins my professional image." He winked.

"I did, thank you. I really appreciate your help. And I know you didn't have to do it, but it also makes me that much more confident I'm working for the right company. A company with heart." Grace started to pack up Holly's belongings.

"Let's not spread the word. I'll have every single parent within a hundred-mile radius trying to work here and bring their baby to work while they do it." Ryan shook his head, not wanting to even think about such a situation.

"My lips are sealed." Grace zipped two fingers across her mouth.

"I'll be out of the office the next couple of days, so you're on your own," Ryan said, grinning at her playfulness.

Chapter Nine

♥

GRACE HADN'T BOTHERED TO tell Ryan she'd fired her sister and he was none the wiser she'd brought the baby to work in his absence, not even bothering to try and find someone. The weekend would have been a good time to find a babysitter, but Spring Fling would complicate those efforts. And then there were the signs she'd offered to pick up from the printers and drop off at the ski resort. So much to do, so little time to do it, and all she really wanted was to have fun with the baby.

"I hope you're going to be a good girl for me today, Holly. We're going to a festival. I'm sure there are lots of neat things I can show you there if the boss man gives me some time away from the booth." Grace smiled at Holly as she tried to grab her necklace and pull it toward her mouth. Drool poured from the sides of her tiny pink lips. Grace reached for a dry cloth to dab the baby's chin. Babies drooled, she got that. But this was extra drooly, and it kept soaking her bibs and shirts, which in turn meant extra clothes and washing at the end of the day.

She considered taking her to the doctor, but it wasn't like she had any legal authorization. Something else Karen had failed to take care of before she left in such a hurry. And Grace's multiple calls to her cousin, had so far, gone unreturned. If it continued, or the baby got fussier, Grace would call her own mother, but until that happened, she was trying to manage on her own.

She loaded the diaper bag with everything imaginable, the overflow landing in a bigger handbag than what she was used to carrying. Grace had more stuff to tote with her than an airline would allow for carry-on and personal baggage without extra charge. She couldn't imagine packing for more than a day trip anywhere. It gave her a healthy appreciation of mothers who managed it all and made it look easy.

"Ready to go, missy?" She flung her handbag over her shoulder along with the diaper bag, carrying Holly on her other hip as they headed for the door. Lucky followed, a hopeful look in her big eyes. "Sorry, girl. Not this time. Maybe we can go for a nice long walk later today." Overloaded, Grace had to forgo petting the dog before she left but promised herself to give her an extra treat tonight.

Running ten minutes behind schedule, Ryan would just have to deal with it. Grace pulled into the parking lot, searching for an empty space. She found one that wasn't exactly close, but it would have to do. She unbuckled Holly from her car seat, tossed the diaper bag and oversized tote over her shoulder, and started the trek toward the rows and rows of tents.

Having no idea where the booth was located, she took a deep breath, and started with the first row. She checked both sides, searching for the World Sport booth. There was a good turnout this year, some booths displaying their crafts or wares for sale, and others advertising their services to everyone who passed by.

Food lines were beginning to get long as people stopped for fried dough, snow cones, cotton candy, and a wide variety of other festival favorites. Grace readjusted her load, the baby getting heavier and heavier by the minute. Another five minutes passed before she spotted the World Sport booth at the end of the second row.

"There you are. I was beginning to think you would be a no-show," Ryan said, his welcome less than perfect, but his quick help to take Holly appreciated.

"Trust me, I considered it. But I value my job, and an order is an order." Grace smiled, hoping to take the sting out of her words. Ryan didn't understand the situation at all, but it wasn't his fault. Normally, she would have been all over the chance to prove herself when it came to her job, especially to a new boss. But that wasn't the case this weekend.

"I didn't realize you were bringing Holly. I take it your sister didn't make it again?" He asked the question, not even bothering to look at Grace, his full attention wrapped up in the baby and tickling her neck and legs.

For a man who professed to have no interest in kids, he sure seemed comfortable with Holly. Another reason to stay away from Ryan, aside from the boss thing. He might come across as a no-family kind of man, but Grace saw things differently. It was hard to miss the connection he was forming with Holly.

"I didn't ask her. She made her position known, and I'm working on finding a replacement. Something I'd be doing today if I weren't here. But since it is my day off, I didn't see any reason I shouldn't be able to bring Holly." Grace dropped the bags off toward the back of the tent and began to inspect the setup.

Someone walked up to the booth and picked up a brochure. "So, who is World Sport Inc., and where are they located?" the lady asked.

"I'll let you explain it while I tend to Holly." Ryan grinned, stepping back from the table.

Grace smile at the woman and dove right into the sales pitch. "It's a new company that's going to take the world of sports equipment and clothing to a new level. Everything related to sports, from equipment and accessories to clothes, can be found in one place, one website. And all with free shipping and returns, and typically one and two-day delivery service. They also have full technical support for every product—something no other online retailer is currently providing at this scale." It helped that Grace believed in Ryan's vision for the company's future, her excitement showing as she rattled off the information.

"But what if I want to try something on? Where are the stores?" The woman's brow scrunched as she tried to understand.

"There will be a handful of signature stores across the nation within a couple of years. But the beauty of World Sport is that your home becomes the store. You can try things on in your own home and return them if you don't like them or they don't fit. With a short shipping time, people can have items go back and forth and pick exactly what's right for them. And if they need something in a hurry but aren't sure what size, they can order two and return one. One-stop shopping without ever leaving your house."

"That sounds amazing. I already do most of my shopping online. Clothes, not so much. But I like the idea of an online sports company dedicated to all things athletic. I look forward to doing business with you all." The woman nodded and grabbed a card.

"Have a nice day. And be sure to tell your friends about us," Grace added, remembering word of mouth was ten times faster than the internet.

"Oh, I will. I noticed your daughter is teething, you might want to try teething biscuits if you haven't already. Worked wonders with my babies."

Teething? Why hadn't she thought of that? Because she wasn't an experienced mom. It made perfect sense. "Thanks for the tip. I hadn't tried that yet." She was trying not to sound surprised. She didn't want Ryan to realize how clueless she really was when it came to babies.

"You're welcome. I noticed the drool is all. You two are blessed to have such a sweet baby. She looks just like her father."

"Thank you, but she's not our baby. I mean, we're not together. He—" she pointed in Ryan's direction "—and I. The baby is with me." She was making a complete mess of something so simple.

"I see. Nice man. Not every guy is a natural with a baby."

Grace turned back to look at what she was seeing. "*Hmmm.* He does have a way with her." Ryan was walking around with the baby and pointing out objects to keep her entertained. Obviously, Grace wasn't the only one who noticed they looked like father and daughter.

"You should snap that man right up if he's single." The woman laughed before wandering off.

Ryan approached. "Well done. Apparently, your marketing creativity extends to selling brand awareness verbally as well. I'm impressed." Between his cologne and his closeness and his flattering words, Grace found herself caught up in the moment. A man-woman moment if there ever was one. Correction, with Holly reaching out to hug her, it was a man-woman-baby moment.

Grace laughed. "I have many talents you are unaware of."

"I look forward to discovering them," Ryan said, handing her the baby.

"Next one's yours. I'm curious what your hidden talents are." It was Grace who had the last laugh, seeing the look of shock on his face. Apparently, the man wasn't used to people challenging him, at least, not when it came to work. But then he didn't know subtlety was not one of her strengths.

The afternoon passed by rather quickly, the two of them taking turns with customers and with Holly. They worked together as a team, each one taking breaks from the booth to parade Holly around. At other times, they let her take center stage as the people who stopped by the booth fell in love with her antics. At one year old, she was quite the character.

A couple of ladies approached, and Grace was surprised to find her mother one of them.

"Mom, I can't believe you're here. This is a great surprise."

"Some of the nurses from Lancaster General planned on coming and insisted I join them. For once, I was inclined to agree. The house is a bit tense right now with everything going on." Her mother exuded confidence, her perfectly coiffured hair and designer linen pantsuit proclaiming her a woman of the world and someone used to getting her way. Except when it came to Faith.

"Trust me, she needed to get away. Too many hours at the pediatric clinic and not enough time for herself," one of her mother's friends confided.

"There's the little darling," her mother said, spotting Holly and Ryan behind her. "I wondered if you'd bring her." Her mom stepped around the table and reached to take the baby from Ryan. "Have you been a good girl, Holly?" Her mother kissed the baby's cheek, Holly laughing and grabbing at the flower in her mother's fancy updo.

Grace realized everything she should have told Ryan could very well come out here and now. Her mother had no idea what was going on. She held her breath, unable to stop whatever was going to happen. She'd just have to deal with it, the same way she always dealt with trouble. Head on.

"Ladies, I'd like you to meet Holly," her mother said proudly, showing her off to her friends.

"She's adorable. I can see why you have pictures of her in your office," one of the women said as she took Holly's hand.

"My sister, Judith, has been good about keeping me in the loop with the most recent pictures."

Ryan's questioning look worried her.

Grace glared at her mother, willing her to let the matter drop. First thing Monday morning she'd tell Ryan, but now wasn't the time or place.

Her mother frowned. "Grace, not to change the subject, but have you talked to your sister yet?"

"No, why?"

"You were a little rough on her and I think you should call to smooth things over." Her mother continued to smile at Holly as she delivered the unwelcome message.

Obviously, nothing had changed. Faith was still her mother's little girl. "What do you mean? She's the one who bailed on me and left me in the lurch. *Twice.*"

"The first time, maybe. But the second time wasn't her fault. She feels bad, but she's even more hurt that you didn't believe she had car trouble. Faith's got a lot of growing up to do but lying has never been one of her faults. Call her, please?" Her mother was right. Maybe she should have been more understanding or patient, or at the very least, listened to what Faith had to say.

"Sure thing, Mom. It was good to see you again. Maybe I'll swing by the house tomorrow and talk to her."

Her mother leaned in to kiss her cheek and handed the baby back. "You do that, I'd love to see you and Holly again when we have more time. By the way, she needs her diaper changed. There's a certain odor coming from her backside if you know what I mean." She grinned before turning to the others as they walked away to the next booth.

Ryan moved to stand next to her. "That was interesting. It sounds like your sister bailed with good cause, and you didn't take the time to listen? That's not the Grace I've come to know, who seems to be fair and balanced most of the time."

Grace bristled at the censure in his voice, feeling guilty enough without Ryan adding a huge topping of condemnation on the top. "You've never let your sister explain, either. How is that any different? What if her reasons are justifiable?"

Ryan tensed. His brow lines were drawn into deep grooves as he tried to come to terms with her accusation. Served him right for butting in where he didn't belong.

A customer walked up, ending their conversation. "You take this one, I've got to change Holly unless you want to volunteer for that duty?"

"Hardly. That's where I draw the line."

"I thought as much." She grinned, walking away and leaving him to take care of the newcomer.

Ryan went into tell-and-sell mode, explaining World Sport's intent. When the customer left, it gave him a chance to think about Grace's comment. He didn't like having his own words thrown back at him, mainly because there was an inkling of truth to them. Bella had left him and never looked back, but what were her reasons? Maybe he owed her that much. Her desertion was one of the reasons he wasn't into relationships or family, but what if everything he believed had been based on a lie?

And Grace and Holly were tied up in answer, whether he wanted them to be or not. He loved it when Holly smiled at him, her antics making him laugh often. Ryan had even grown used to having her around and would miss her sweet face when Grace found childcare. At that point, he'd be relegated to office parties and pictures to watch Holly grow up. The idea did not sit well.

Neither did the idea of tamping down any growing feelings toward Grace that kept cropping up, demanding attention. She'd been appropriately named, for sure. The woman was full of grace, giving credit to her name, and it radiated to all those around her every day.

Only the knowledge of what happened when you got close to someone kept him at bay. The last thing he wanted was to open himself up to a repeat of the pain he'd experienced as a child. It had the power to destroy him, his financial future, and that of those who'd entrusted him to make this venture successful.

He thought he wasn't into family and children, but he was wrong. He thought he wasn't into relationships, but he was wrong. The question then came to mind, what else could he be wrong about? But the truth was, it didn't matter. Too much was riding on the outcome to be sidetracked for fleeting feelings for a woman and her daughter.

Determined to stay the course, Ryan renewed his vow to stay away from Grace and the temptation she presented for a normal, happy life. Maybe it was time to close the chapter of his past with Bella, proving Grace wrong, and providing him with a solid reason why family life wasn't for him.

Chapter Ten

♥

SUNLIGHT STREAMED THROUGH THE slightly tilted blinds, letting Grace know morning had come, and with it, an entire day with Holly to have fun. She glanced at the sleeping baby next to her, the result of Grace giving into her fussy cries last night. How could she resist those big blue eyes or the fact she liked being able to snuggle with Holly? The fresh scent of a baby after a bath was one that would never grow old.

Lucky was perched at the end of the bed, her new normal spot. After getting over her initial fit of jealousy, it would appear the dog had designated herself protector of the household. The end of the bed strategically placed her between Grace and the portable crib.

Grace edged out of bed, careful not to wake the baby. She pushed the blankets up and around Holly, stacking pillows like fortress walls to barricade around her. With a few extra pillows strategically placed on the floor, Grace grabbed the monitor and headed to the kitchen for a much-needed cup of coffee. Lucky, on the other hand, laid her head back down, choosing to play guard over the baby.

The past week had gone by incredibly fast, and with so many ups and downs, that Grace barely had a chance to experience the joy of parenthood. Just because it was temporary, didn't mean she couldn't savor it. She tightened her robe and settled in at the table, savoring the warm chicory flavor.

Church services started at nine-thirty, giving Grace plenty of time to get ready. The baby wasn't registered for childcare at the church, but Grace didn't mind, much preferring to keep Holly with her. Plenty of parents brought their children to church successfully, and so could she.

And after church, Grace couldn't wait to take Holly to the park. She glanced at the phone, her mother's words coming back to her. *"Talk to your sister."*

Might as well get it over with. Grace picked up the phone and pressed the speed dial for Faith.

"Do you know what time it is?" Her sister's sleepy voice reminded her it was early.

"Sorry. I just wanted to tell you I was sorry for cutting you off the other day. I was hasty in my judgment." It hadn't been a good day for Grace. Her motto of *quick to listen, slow to speak, and slow to anger* had gone out the proverbial window, and in its place, she'd been left with regret. More proof the motto was a good one to live by.

"Mom told you, right?"

"Yes. I am sorry. I've been super stressed with the new job and trying to manage taking care of Holly. I know it's not a good excuse, but I want to make it up to you." Grace needed to go the extra mile to make amends.

"I'm listening." Faith wasn't going to give in easily, but it was understandable.

"Why don't you meet me at church today in Hallbrook? Then afterward, we can lunch at O'Malley's, my treat, of course, and then we can go to the park. It'll be a fun day and give us a chance to hang. Have some sister time." Getting Faith to church would be a good move. She knew her sister probably hadn't gone in years.

"I'm not much of a church fan, and you're forgetting, I don't have a car." She wasn't going to let Grace off the hook that easy.

"Get Mom to come. I'd love to see you both. It'll be fun. Please, Faith. Give me the chance to make it up to you. You know how much I love you and hate it when we can't even talk. We've never been close, but I think we should change that, don't you?" The words rang true, even if they had been spontaneous. Maybe it was time to get to know Faith better, after all, they were both adults.

"Fine. I've got nothing else to do today," Faith's answer came out reluctantly, but at least she'd agreed. It was a big step in the right direction.

"What's going on with your car?" Grace asked, showing interest as a gesture of goodwill.

"It's the starter or something like that. It's a couple hundred bucks to repair, and I don't have anywhere close to that much money. How I'm supposed to earn an income when I don't have wheels is beyond me." She could sense Faith's frustration.

What made it worse was that her sister was right. It was a double-edged sword.

"Come stay with me. I offered before, but now it makes perfect sense and is a great solution to both our problems."

"What do you mean?"

"You babysit Holly until Karen comes back to take her home, and I'll make sure you have enough money to fix your car and have a few dollars extra in your pocket." By then, she would have her first paycheck, and it would solve her childcare issue once and for all. It was the perfect plan.

Her sister's silence was a good sign. Grace waited, letting her come to the right decision on her own.

"Promise?" Faith asked, letting out a deep enough sigh that Grace could hear it over the phone.

Good choice, sis. "Yes. Bring whatever you need when we meet, and then you can ride home with me."

"It's a deal. And, Grace, I really did feel bad calling out on you after I promised."

"I know, kiddo. Let's just forget it. Look on the bright side, I still have my job." Grace wanted to start over, and that meant putting things behind them, not rehashing the past.

"You must be amazing to be able to do your job and take care of the baby. Either that or your boss is super into you,' Faith added, her voice tinged with laughter.

Attracted to her, maybe. But into her? Absolutely not. The two were completely different things. One was based on physical awareness, while the other was based on emotional and personal connections. "I must be good at my job because Ryan has no interest. Trust me."

He'd made his stance perfectly clear, especially when she'd butted into his personal relationship with his sister. She'd obviously crossed a line. Holly was another matter altogether. Ryan was clearly growing more attached. The man was made to be a father, if only he could see it.

"*Hmmm*. Interesting," Faith murmured.

"What?" Grace asked, unsure what her sister meant.

"You didn't say anything about your interest in him." Faith had it all wrong.

"Because there's nothing to mention." It was true. Physical awareness counted for nothing in Grace's books. Okay, well, something. But there was more to it than that, and relationships were overrated anyway.

"You're telling me there's nothing at all between you?" Faith persisted.

"Nothing."

"The man must be a saint. Or there's something wrong with him."

Grace shook her head and smiled. "Saint Ryan. I'll tell him you said that when he's having one of his super-tense moments. At least that nickname is better than Vomit Man."

"Do I even want to know?" Faith asked, the curiosity in her voice obvious. This was the first real conversation Grace could remember having with her sister in a very long time. It was nice.

"Probably not, but I'll tell you the story after church. It'll make a great conversation for the park. I hear the baby stirring, and I need to get a move on. I'll meet you at nine-twenty outside the front of the church. Ciao, sister."

"*Ciao.*"

An hour later, Grace arrived at the church and spotted her mother and Faith right where they agreed to meet. And on time, wonder of wonders. Of course, Grace, on the other hand, was a little late, but she was getting better and better at the timing thing with each day that passed.

"Good morning," she said, addressing her mother and sister as she approached. Grace leaned in to kiss her mother's cheek. She'd have to remember to check her own cheek for lipstick marks. Her mother was one of those women who laid the waxy color on dark and thick. Dressed to the nines, her mother's matching jacket and skirt were more formal than the modern mode of comfortable and casual.

Faith, on the other hand, had no such qualms about how she dressed. Her blue jeans and T-shirt were the exact opposite of their mother. Grace had learned to land somewhere in the middle.

"Good morning, Grace. This is a first. I don't recall you ever being late for anything." Her mother grinned, reaching for Holly.

"Morning," Faith said, moving to stand next to their mother, intent on talking baby talk to Holly.

"I've never had to take care of a baby before. Oh, my goodness. How did you manage to do it and work a full-time job? And single parents. Wow. They deserve a medal for figuring out how to manage a crazy life." Grace readjusted the diaper bag and her sweater, everything askew from carrying the baby.

"Single parent's need to rely more on a great support team and be very organized. With two parents, it wasn't easy, but your father and I managed. We juggled the schedules the best we could, and some of the time, things didn't work out so well. Of course, when Faith came along, we had you."

"Except you didn't trust me with your porcelain-doll baby until I was like fifteen. I remember begging you to let me babysit." Grace started up the stairs to the church.

"It was a problem pregnancy, not to mention a late one. I never meant to upset you, but I became more protective than necessary."

That was an understatement. "I know. I just like to give you grief. But hey, it gave me more free time to study, and my efforts all paid off." Grace had resented her mother's lack of trust, but in hindsight, it had been a blessing. Her grades and acceptance into college on a scholarship had all come as a result of applying herself.

They entered the small white church and took seats toward the back, just in case Holly started to fuss. Taking turns holding the baby and keeping her entertained, the three of them listened to the message.

Today was about forgiveness, appropriate considering her and Faith's situation. Too bad Ryan wasn't here to listen to the sermon. He could use more wisdom in the area of forgiveness, at least when it came to his sister.

The hour of sermon and song passed quickly, and soon they were talking with everyone who stopped to find out about the baby. Grace flushed with pleasure as she introduced Holly, loving the attention a baby brought to the mix.

The sun was shining, and it was a beautiful day for a walk, and they all decided to head for the park first. Karen had left her a stroller, and after strapping Holly in, they followed the sidewalk that wound through the park passed some of the flowering bushes. Pink and red azaleas predominately decorated the place, like a breath of fresh air, welcoming summer just around the corner. The place was overrun with families, everyone having the same idea and wanting to enjoy the warmer weather.

"So, what's going on with you and your boss? What's with the subterfuge?" her mother asked when they stopped in front of the playground.

"Thanks for not outing me, by the way. It's just, one thing led to another, and he assumed she was my daughter. It was easier to let him believe she was mine. I worried he'd be a lot less understanding if he knew I was watching someone else's baby and bringing the baby to work." Grace unstrapped Holly and carried her to the plastic swing designed for toddlers.

"I see what you mean, but you should tell him. You've been there a week now, and if he hasn't fired you yet, he's not going to."

Faith pushed the swing as Holly clapped and giggled, enjoying the attention.

"I know. I'm sure things will quiet down this coming week since Faith's watching the baby, and I'll find a way to tell him." After Holly left was preferable, but probably not the best option.

"He seemed like a nice man." Her mother's gaze landed on Grace.

"He is. And although he'd never admit it, I think he enjoys Holly's attention. She seems taken with him."

"Single?" her mother asked.

"What is it with you and Faith? One-track minds. He's single and plans to remain that way if you must know." Everyone wanted to marry her off, but it wasn't that easy. It's not that she didn't want to get married, it was finding the right guy that was the problem. And she wasn't willing to risk her heart over and over to have it pounced on. There was only so much a person could take before the heartbreak did permanent damage.

"Don't get so defensive. It's just been a while since you dated. Maybe Ryan planned to remain single because he hadn't met you yet, sweetheart. You have to think positively." Her mother always assumed the best. Anything less wasn't acceptable.

"Wishful thinking." Grace laughed. "You know it won't work for me, and you know why. I've been through it before. Twice. I won't do it again." She wanted to have a good day, not talk about her short-comings.

"The right guy won't care," her mother pressed the issue.

"I'm not dating anyone and putting my heart on the line again, hoping to find a needle in the haystack. Most men want a kid to carry on their name." Grace started to walk away, intent on ending the conversation.

"So why is he against relationships?" her mother asked, following her.

Grace shrugged. "He's a workaholic with a family grudge, the way I see it."

"Sounds perfect."

"I don't follow you." Grace frowned.

"Maybe he's not into having a family, but what if he's into you? Maybe there's room for compromise. Two people who work hard during the day and enjoy each other's company at night."

"You are living in some fairy tale romance be-cause you and Dad found what most people want. It's not that easy, and it doesn't always happen that way."

"It can. Never say never. Just keep your heart open to the possibilities. I saw the way he looked at you when you weren't watching. The man was interested."

He was? Her mother must be mistaken. Grace was interested all right, but being interested and brave enough to put her heart and soul on the line again? *Not a chance.*

The three of them laughed and joked, each one trying to outdo the other in vying for the baby's attention. Holly's short little legs didn't seem to slow down her fast crawl across the grass. Her bubbly sounds and baby giggles, along with the antics of her discovering new things, kept them all highly entertained. It was nice to see her sister joining in the fun, and her mother captured several great snapshots. It was a day to remember for sure.

Grace picked up Holly and twirled her like a helicopter, much to the baby's delight. She hugged her tightly.

"Mama," Holly said, yanking at the chain around Grace's neck.

Grace beamed, looking up at the others to see if they were paying attention. "Did you hear that? Did you?"

"I heard baba. She must be hungry." Faith's smirk meant she'd heard precisely what Holly said.

"No. I heard her right. She just called me mama." The truth suddenly dawned on Grace—sucking the air out of her chest. She wasn't Holly's mother. That honor belonged to Karen. Her cousin would be heart-broken to have missed her first word. "You're probably right, it was just baba," she said, trying to downplay the situation.

Faith looked at her mother and shrugged.

"Honey, you're her mama for the next two weeks. Enjoy it. If anyone deserves it, it's you."

Her mother's words caused her to tear up and Grace brushed them away, just as her mother pulled her into a hug. Something she desperately needed.

After one week, she was madly in love with Holly. *What would happen after three weeks?*

Chapter Eleven

♥

RYAN STAYED BUSY DURING the grand opening. Between overseeing the orders, helping the employees to keep things running smoothly, and ensuring that every order was pulled correctly and shipped out in a timely fashion, it had required long hours in the warehouse.

The whole process was designed to be easy. Still, this early in the game, it was critical the company upheld their promises to customers. It was all about building a reputation and getting the word out at this point. The team had embraced the concept he'd founded the company upon, each one dedicated to make World Sport, Inc. a massive success.

And as to getting noticed, well, that was Grace's responsibility. Something she'd done with flying colors all week. The ads she'd sent him for approval were both dynamic and eye-catching. Without Holly in the office, it was a whole lot less chaotic, but also a lot quieter. He missed the little tyke, much as he was loath to admit it.

The biggest advantage of working in the warehouse, however, had been that it kept him out of the office, and therefore, he'd managed to keep Grace off his radar. The attractive blonde had occupied far too many of his thoughts lately, thoughts that should be focused solely on the company. The bigger problem, however, was a far stronger reason to stay away. She was his employee, and not one he was willing to risk losing. It didn't stop him from looking forward to seeing her fresh face and smile each morning, but that's as far as he would let it go.

All week, the steady pace of orders had rolled in, keeping him hopeful the business would be a smashing success. Anxious for Grace to compile the sales data, he'd broke down and asked her to expedite the report and complete it over the weekend. He was like Charlie opening a candy bar to find the golden ticket for Willy Wonka's Chocolate Factory. But once he'd asked, he felt better. Especially considering she'd agreed to work on it after church, totally understanding his impatience.

He clicked on the button to refresh his email server, unsure when Grace would finish the report. But he had another reason for the constant email checks, one he hadn't told a single soul about. After hours and hours of deliberation, mostly to talk himself out of it, Ryan had hit the send button to reply to the foster care agency regarding his sister. There was no way to know how long it would take for the process to move to the next step, but he was as nervous about hearing from Bella as he was about getting the numbers from Grace. His life was in a state of turmoil now, something he wasn't used to. But he also felt more alive than he had in a long time.

His phone rang, Jordan's name popping up on the screen. "What's up?" he answered, cutting the formalities with his partner.

"Any word on the numbers?" Jordan had every right to be nervous, his partner having invested a considerable sum of money.

"Not yet. You'll be the first to know, followed shortly by the investors. Grace promised me she'd pull the reports today, and she will. She hasn't let me down yet."

"I still can't believe you let her bring a baby to work. Asking for trouble, in my opinion." Jordan had given him a fair amount of grief over the issue, but in the end, he'd backed down for the same reasons Ryan had. They needed her.

"For your information, she has childcare now, and it was only the first week. And judging from what I've seen, you did a great job hiring her, and it was just a small hiccup that we all got through."

"Glad to hear it. We have too much tied to this venture to have anything go wrong." Jordan was right. Everyone who had believed in him and his plan stood to lose if this didn't fly the way the forecast models had shown.

"I agree. Hang on, I just got an email notification. Let me check while you're on the line." Ryan tapped the buttons to bring up his mail account.

From: Grace Baxter

Subject: Grand-Opening Numbers

He scanned the document, dropping his gaze to the bottom line number that reflected the total sales for the week. Better than any projections or expectations they'd had. He let out the breath he'd been holding and forwarded the email to his partner.

"Well, how does it look?" Jordan asked.

"Hang on, I'm going over it now. I forwarded it to you, but my first impression is a good one. A really good one." It seemed hard to believe, but the numbers don't lie. "This is cause for a celebration."

"Really? I like the sound of that." The tension had gone out of Jordan's voice.

"We exceeded our initial goals by almost twenty percent." Ryan shook his head, floored by the numbers, still finding it hard to believe.

"Yes," Jordan exclaimed. "The man with the golden touch has struck again. I sure am glad you brought me along for the ride. Shoot the numbers to the investors. It'll buy us a lot of time with this kind of profit margins the first week out. All we have to do now is keep the ball rolling. If we don't let up on the marketing and keep pushing the name and concept, our customer base will continue to grow and eat into our competitor's share exponentially. Let's celebrate next week. I'll come to town, and we can go to dinner."

"Sounds like a plan." Except Ryan felt like celebrating tonight. The numbers were a big deal, and he wanted to bask in the good news. Without giving it too much thought, Ryan called Grace. Who better to share it with than someone who completely understood the huge success the numbers represented?

She answered on the first ring. "Hey there. I got the email. I can't thank you enough for compiling the information today. And I promise, no more Sunday work. It was fantastic news, and I've sent the report on to my partner and the investors."

"That's what you said about last weekend when I had to work Spring Fling," she teased. "Seriously, I'm glad I could help. If it had been next Sunday, you can be sure I would have told you no, so consider yourself lucky."

"Next Sunday? What's so special that makes it off-limits? Besides my promise not to make you work weekends anymore."

"Mother's Day. Why is it that men always forget special holidays?"

"I don't know about most men, but in my case, I haven't celebrated that day since I was seven. Trust me, it's better to forget." Ryan had spent the last twenty-two years trying to forget, but now, thanks to Grace he was remembering. But it was a good memory. The last drawing he'd made for his mother. Her smile had been like sunshine on a cloudy day, the love in her eyes genuine. He'd given her a moment of joy in what turned out to be her final days. Maybe that was half his problem. Ryan should have focused on the good times with his parents, not the miserable aftermath.

"I'm sorry, I didn't mean to—"

"Don't worry. My mother was very sick before she passed away. It was a long time ago." It would have been easier to laugh off Grace's comment and play dumb, but for some reason, with her, he couldn't do it. She invoked shared confidences he wasn't used to.

And even more reason to change the subject. "Listen, your ads made all the difference. The changes you made were insightful and spot on. I want to celebrate the success, and I think you should celebrate with me. Tonight." Ryan stopped pacing and waited. It wouldn't be like a date. Just a boss and employee toasting the company's success—at least the way he saw it.

"Tonight?" Grace asked, her tone incredulous.

"Yes. A business dinner. Is Faith still there to watch Holly?" He preferred an adult dinner, but he also missed the baby, and having her around wouldn't be so bad. Not to mention, it would make it less date like.

"Yes, but I don't know if that's such a good idea." Neither did he, but he wasn't running away. It was just business.

"Her watching the baby tonight, or you coming to dinner with me?" he asked, realizing her comment could be taken a couple of ways.

"The latter. I don't want to complicate things. Between us," Grace said, her voice dropping low. He wasn't used to her being unsure of herself.

"It's a celebratory business dinner. Nothing complicated about it. I realize we are both mature adults who happened to be attracted to one another." It was easier to admit than he thought it would be, but he hoped a straightforward disclosure would lend itself to keeping things on the level. "But it doesn't mean we have to do anything about it. The boss-employee line is clearly cut in the proverbial sand." *And in the employee manual.*

"Okay, then. As long as we are on the same page. This job is important to me, and I wouldn't want the boss to fire me over something like this. I'm already walking a fine line with him," Grace teased, the sound of her laughter like music.

"You're not going to get fired. Trust me. You're great at your job, and I don't want to lose you, so there is that. I'll pick you up at six. Is that okay?" Ryan's heart raced in double-time, the idea of spending the evening in Grace's company far more pleasing than it should be.

"Any idea where you want to go?" she asked.

"That's up to you. We can stay in town if you prefer, maybe go to O'Malley's Charm? I totally understand if you don't want to be far away from Holly. You're a good mother, Grace." In fact, she was just like his mother, from what he remembered before she died.

"About that... There's something I've been meaning to tell you," Grace said, the hesitation in her voice catching his attention.

Ryan's phone beeped with another incoming call. "Hold that thought. I've got another call coming in. Why don't you tell me tonight?" Judging by whatever it was, it had to be important and in person might be better anyway.

"Okay."

"Thanks. Got to run." He pressed the end button and switched the call to the other line. "Hey, Larry. Did you get my email?" Larry was one of the largest investors and controlled a lot of the board's decisions.

"I did, which is why I'm calling. I wanted to tell you how pleased we are. I hope next week's ads are just as exciting and continue to bring in the business. It's rare to exceed goals in the first week of a start-up."

"I've been reviewing and approving them all week. Grace is a dynamite ad exec, and we were fortunate to get her."

"Excellent." They talked for another five minutes, but then he heard a woman call Larry's name. "That's the wife. Got to go."

"Gotcha. Goodnight." Ryan felt a tug in his heart. Larry had a loving wife and two daughters. Family.

Something Ryan had always vowed to never have in his life, and yet the familiar pang struck at odd times. *Like now.*

He glanced at his watch and realized he needed to jump in the shower and change right away if he didn't want to be late picking up Grace. It took him less than twenty minutes, but he resisted the urge to show up early, knowing it wouldn't look right to act like an overzealous suitor showing up at her door.

Grace tried on several outfits for her so-called business dinner, settling on jeans and a coral blouse, adding coral earrings and a white beaded necklace to spruce it up. Simple yet dressy.

It had surprised Grace when Ryan admitted he was attracted to her, but his off-limits declaration—that was totally expected. She agreed it was better, all things considered. Unfortunately, her heart wasn't totally on board with their mutual decision.

Grace finished applying the last touches of make-up just as the doorbell rang, announcing Ryan's arrival. Lucky barked and ran out of the room, determined to check out who was visiting.

"I'll get it," Faith hollered. Her sister had been amazing this past week, helping whenever and however she could. It was as though she'd grown up overnight. Grace could only hope it lasted when the job was over. Her sister had taken to Holly, and clearly, Holly felt the same adoration. The baby followed Faith around everywhere, to the point Grace was almost jealous and wished she didn't have to go to the office every day.

Grace could hear Ryan and Faith talking in the front room, Ryan's deep voice carrying down the hall. A shiver of excitement washed over her. He'd been clear it was just business tonight, but part of her wanted to imagine what it would be like to be his date. A real date.

"The man cares about you." Her mother's words came back to her, but in this instance, her mother was wrong. Okay, so maybe only partly wrong. But attraction was not caring. Ryan didn't do relationships, something he'd made clear. Repeatedly.

Grace spritzed on her favorite perfume and headed for the living room She drew up short as she entered, surprised to see Ryan holding the baby, talking and laughing. Dressed in khaki slacks, a dress shirt, and a blue sport coat, he looked totally GQ, his wavy curls adding a touch of boyishness to his appearance. The man was a natural charmer, and Holly and Faith were clearly charmed, judging by the rapt attention he was receiving.

She'd forgotten to remind Faith not to say anything about Karen and hoped the subject hadn't come up. Grace planned on telling Ryan the truth tonight. She was tired of covering her bases, and clearly, he wasn't going to fire her over the situation. Especially now that Faith was taking care of Holly every day. At least, she would be for another week.

The idea of Holly leaving soon was enough to kick Grace's good attitude in the backside, serving as a dose of reality. But at least she'd have Holly for Mother's Day. Karen wasn't due to arrive until the Tuesday after. It wouldn't seem like much to most people, but to Grace, having the baby here for Mother's Day was like winning the lottery. Or better.

"Hey, there. Looks like someone's having fun," Grace said, smiling at the relaxed scene in front of her.

"She's hard to resist." Ryan looked in Grace's direction, appreciation in his expression.

Wishful thinking on Grace's part had her imagining it was a double-entendre and that he was including her in the comment.

"You should have seen Holly," her sister said, laughing. "The minute she spotted Ryan, she squealed and went crawling to him. Suddenly, I was like minced meat, and he was the mashed potatoes with gravy on top."

Ryan frowned. "Interesting analogy."

Grace shook her head and grinned. "It's something my mother always said when something better came along."

"I see." He smiled, twirling Holly around in his arms, making her giggle. The man was a natural with children. "Beautiful dog, by the way."

"Her name's Lucky. She's a roan-springer-spaniel mix, or at least that's what the rescue center told me. I fell in love with her coloring, big ears, big paws, and long fur. Although, the dog hair can be a bit much at times." Grace laughed.

Ryan put one hand out for Lucky to sniff, letting her get to know him. It wasn't long before the dog started wagging her tail, and Grace knew her canine friend approved of the hunky guy. "We probably should get going," he said, finally putting Holly down. "You look nice, by the way. If I'm allowed to compliment you on this business date." He winked.

Her heart raced a little faster. The compliment had been delivered smoothly but effectively, judging by the ripples of pleasure easing down her spine. "It's allowed. And thank you."

Grace turned to her sister. "Make sure Holly's in bed by eight. I'm trying to keep her on a schedule."

"What for? Why not have fun while we can?" Faith shrugged.

Grace glared at her sister, trying to remind her who was standing in the room. This wasn't how she envisioned Ryan finding out. She preferred to ease him into the knowledge. "Because she needs structure. There is a time and place for fun, and it's not after bedtime. Call me on my cell if you need me.

Oh, and can you feed Lucky?" Grace headed for the front door with Ryan not far behind.

"Fine. Come on, kiddo. We've only got a couple hours to play before the battle-ax says you have to go to beddy-by." Faith scooped up Holly, helping her to wave goodbye.

"Thanks," Grace said dryly.

As soon as the door closed behind them, Ryan took her by the arm and led her to his car. There was nothing business-like about the move, but Grace opted to remain quiet.

Chapter Twelve

♥

G RACE WAS A LITTLE nervous now that they were in the car and on their way to dinner. The last time they'd been this close, they'd gone to the ski resort on a business trip, but nothing about this felt like business.

"Jordan is pretty excited about the numbers, as am I. You're a marketing genius." At least Ryan was steering the conversation away from Holly and back to business. It would make things easier.

"I would have to say it's more to do with the concept. The idea you came up with is incredible. I'm sure other companies will soon jump in and follow suit." She glanced over at him, observing his strong jawline without a trace of his normal five o'clock shadow at this time of day. Had he showered and shaved for the occasion? The slight hint of woodsy cologne lingering in the car said he had, and the knowledge only served to increase her anticipation of the evening. Business or personal didn't matter—being with Ryan did.

"So now that we have the mutual admiration out-of-the-way, can I just say I'm looking forward to this evening. You've worked hard the past two weeks, despite any setbacks you faced, and you deserve this."

Ryan parked the car and the two of them made their way down the sidewalk to O'Malley's. He opened the door, stepping back to let her enter first. Grace was pleasantly surprised when Agnes O'Malley greeted them. She and her husband owned the place but had retired a few years back. It was their sons who ran the bar and restaurant now.

"It's nice to see you, Mrs. O'Malley. I haven't seen you in a while."

"I finally got Frank to do some traveling." She grinned, picking up two menus. "He won't let on, but I think he enjoys it. Tonight, Seth wasn't feeling well, and I offered to cover for him. Follow me, I've got the perfect table for you two." She winked at Grace and started across the room.

The older woman led them to a corner booth. "Ruth is your server, and I'll send her right over. Enjoy your meal."

"Thank you. This is perfect." *Not.* It was far too intimate and cozy for a business dinner. Mrs. O'Malley walked away, leaving them alone.

"She must think we're a couple. She gave us the most romantic table in the place," Ryan said as he held out a seat for her.

"I agree. But I didn't want to be rude and make her move us. Unfortunately, the Hallbrook gossip line will have us hooked up by morning. When a man and woman go out on the town, it's rarely business." She gazed at him, knowing a lot could be told about a person's true reaction based on facial expression alone. Words could lie, faces rarely did.

"Well, if I have to be the subject of gossip, I doubt I could be attached to a better person." Ryan winked, his eyes crinkling at the corners as his smile deepened. Not an ounce of tension was exhibited to make her doubt his words.

Grace felt a warm flush creep across her face and down her throat. She was grateful for the low lighting that would hide it from Ryan.

After Ruth took their order and left, the two of them talked about the report until the bartender delivered the wine. "Thanks, Jack," Grace said when he finished pouring.

"No problem. Enjoy." The older man smiled and walked away.

Ryan lifted his glass for a toast, clinking the crystal against hers. "Congratulations. Here's to a first great sales week as a team."

"Congratulations. We did make a pretty good team, despite the bumps, or in my case, the baby, along the way." Ryan had been pretty great about Holly and deserved tons of kudos for the fact she'd been able to get her job done. He was turning out to be a fantastic boss, one who truly cared about those who worked for him.

"Let's try to not spend the whole night talking shop."

"*Ummm*, isn't that what people do at business dinners? What do you want to talk about if not work?" She assumed he had a one-track mind and it was always going full speed ahead when it came to the company.

"Well, for starters, your sister."

A most surprising topic. "My sister?"

"Faith seems like a nice girl, and she's very attentive with the baby. Not exactly the way you painted her. Has she changed that much, or is most of this you playing big sister and being tough on her?" Ryan leaned forward, interested in her answer, and not just making small talk.

"Maybe a little bit of both. Faith is capable of so much more, and I want her to do well. I don't see the harm in that. But I have noticed she's gotten very close to Holly this past week. I think being away from her normal run of friends is giving her a chance to focus on other things. I'm hoping perhaps she'll grow up just enough to take on adulthood and move forward with her life." Grace didn't often talk about her family, but Ryan made it easy.

"I'd have to say your week's been successful then."

"What do you mean?" Grace asked, unsure of what he meant.

"Apparently, Faith's planning on enrolling in the nursing program at the community college this fall. She's decided to work in the pediatric ward. I saw nothing but love in her eyes for her niece. Holly has clearly impacted her decisions regarding her future."

Niece? Try cousin. Grace let out a deep breath. His comment reminded her of the decision to fess up tonight, hoping the spirit of celebration would make it easier. "Really? She hasn't said a thing to me about it. Or to my mother, that I know of." There had been plenty of opportunities for Faith to bring it up and she didn't understand her sister's secrecy.

"I get the feeling it's a new decision. Let your sister tell you in her own time. Pretend you didn't hear it from me. But maybe knowing what she's planning will give you some peace of mind that she's moving in the right direction."

"That's awesome. Thank you so much for telling me. I can't wait to tell Mom, but I'll swear her to secrecy until we actually hear it from Faith." Grace nodded and smiled. Ryan was right—it did take a huge weight off her shoulders.

He took a sip of his drink as Ruth returned with their lasagna entrees. The fresh aroma of garlic and tomatoes wafted toward her, reminding her of how hungry she was. The O'Malley's lasagna recipe was known throughout the county, and people came for miles for a serving of the flavorful, saucy, meat and cheese noodles layered and topped with cheese to perfection. Ruth topped off their glasses with more wine, and after making sure they didn't need anything else, headed back toward the kitchen.

Grace's leg shook under the table, knowing the time was at hand for her to tell Ryan the truth. It's not like after next week he wouldn't find out anyway when she suddenly turned up childless. She took a deep breath and tried to calm her nerves. *Please, Lord, help me know what to say and help Ryan to understand why I felt the need to lie.*

She took a deep breath. "Do you remember when we were on the phone earlier today, and I mentioned we needed to talk? And then you got a phone call and said we'd talk tonight."

"I do." Ryan leaned back in his chair; his gaze fixed on her.

Grace rubbed the stem of her wine glass between her thumb and forefinger as if trying to transfer some of her nervous energy to the crystal.

Ryan's phone lit up, vibrating a demand for him to answer. "Sorry. It's Jordan," Ryan said, casting her an apologetic look.

Saved by the phone. Again. "Take it. It's fine." *Maybe it was a sign she needed to keep her mouth shut about the whole thing.*

Ryan took the call. "What's up, Jordan?"

Grace wasn't trying to eavesdrop, but it's not like she had a choice considering she was across the table from him.

"I see. No. I totally agree. If she can't get her personal life in order, there's no place for her on the team. The company is too new for someone to be missing work repeatedly because of problems at home. She has a responsibility to her job as well."

Grace paled at Ryan's words. He wasn't talking about her, but he might as well have been. He'd cut her some slack the first day, but he was clearly not on the human-relations side of understanding when it came to the real-life concerns of his employees. There was no way she could tell him now. What if anything else went wrong? She'd be out on her keister faster than she could spell the word. Holly's parentage was ultimately no concern of anyone's.

"Sorry about that." He shut off the phone. "What is it you wanted to tell me?"

Grace tensed, trying to find something to say. "I just wanted to say thanks for putting up with me and the challenges I faced this week. Your confidence in me makes me realize how much I'm going to enjoy working at World Sport."

"You're welcome. But you've already thanked me numerous times." He shrugged. "This isn't about that call I just took, is it? Jordan said the woman has called in late every morning with a different excuse. With your work ethic, you have nothing to worry about."

"Thanks, but it does bear thinking about. There's no boyfriend or husband to help out if I run into trouble, and since I plan on keeping it that way, I don't have many options."

"Either one of those could change. I'm sure you have guys lined up wanting to take you out. Charles included," Ryan said.

Grace got the feeling he was testing her about Charles, but whether she went out with his friend or not, wasn't any of his business. It's not like Ryan wanted to date her. It was time to steer back the conversation back into neutral territory. "Maybe, maybe not. It doesn't matter because I don't date. I don't need a man." She looked away, not wanting him to read anything into her expression.

"You're a bit young to be cynical against relationships."

"You're one to talk," Grace said, glancing back at him.

Ryan shrugged. "Well, my family hasn't been a great example."

Grace reached out and grabbed his hand. "Tell me what happened, Ryan." They were long past the business line and had moved solidly into personal territory. But at least she'd managed to switch the conversation to be about him.

He looked at her long and hard as if trying to decide how to answer. Or maybe, judging by his expression, whether to answer at all.

"It's not pretty. My mother and father were in love. Like soul mates. And when she got sick, my father worked harder and longer, struggling to hold everything together. When my mother passed away, my father lost a piece of himself. And then he lost his job and our family lost everything. We were homeless for a while, which is something I swore I would never let happen to me again." The pain reflected in his eyes touched her heart.

"But how did you get from there to the foster home you told me about?" She wanted to understand him, to get to know the man, not the boss.

"We were living on the streets. The state stepped in and took us away. My father died not long after that. Honestly, I think he stopped living after my mother passed away. Without her, he didn't feel he had a reason to go on. My sister, Bella, was the only family I had left after that, and then she deserted me. Hard work equals financial stability. There's no room in the equation for family." Ryan sat back in his seat and let out a deep breath. "Aren't you glad you asked?" Ryan added cynically.

His views on family and relationship had been etched in stone at such a young age, his story heartbreaking. But there was more to life than what he was seeing. "I am. And you're wrong about family. Plenty of people have careers and things don't work out. Life isn't always fair. But, it's faith, family, and close friends that can help people through the hard times. People need love. Money won't buy happiness—only love can do that."

"I wouldn't know. Neither my sister, nor my foster parents bothered to show me anything different. I guess what I learned at eight, stuck." Ryan grimaced; lines of tension deeply etched across his forehead.

Grace cared about Ryan and wanted to help him see things differently. "Have you thought about what I suggested regarding Bella? About reconsidering and responding to the email?"

"I have," he nodded, his sudden half-smile catching her off guard. "I was waiting for the right moment to tell you. For better or worse, I answered the email. Happy?"

"Yes, I am. For you. Either way, you'll get the answers you need to move forward. You shut your heart off to the world, and it's not healthy. The world can be a pretty special place if you have someone to share it with."

"Spoken from the woman who just said she wasn't into relationships." He grinned, rolling his eyes to make his point.

"I have my reasons. None of which matter at this point. So, what happens now?" Grace couldn't believe he'd done it. Talk about being brave. Braver than she was, for sure.

"I got a response that said they would reach out and give Bella my contact information. Beyond that, it's up to her if she still wants to communicate. I'm not holding my breath, but I've called her bluff."

"Bluff? I don't think a couple of years of trying to reach out to you is a bluff. Bella wants to see you, and she wants to talk to you. She'll be in touch. Of that, I have no doubt." Grace could only hope now that she'd opened Pandora's box, so to speak, that it didn't come back to bite her and him in the backside. She prayed it would all work out well for Ryan.

"Can we talk about something else? This is supposed to be a celebration, not a night of kiss and tell." Ryan winked as he lifted his wine glass and took a sip.

"We might be telling, but I don't see any kissing." Grace grinned, totally in agreement it was time to lighten the subject. Especially a conversation that now included kissing—something she'd wanted to do since she first met him. Well, almost from the beginning. Holly vomiting on Ryan hadn't made her think of kisses, and neither had finding out Vomit Man was her boss.

They laughed and talked throughout the rest of the dinner, each steering clear of sensitive subjects but finding plenty to talk about. They had a lot in common, and if he weren't so anti-relationship, knowing he was anti-children would've tipped her hand in his favor and made her reconsider agreeing to just be friends.

Grace noticed on the way back to her house that things felt different between them. Yes, they were friends, but contrary to what Ryan said earlier, there was something almost tangible between them that couldn't be denied.

"Let me get the door for you." Ryan put his hand on her shoulder to stop her from exiting the car when she made a move to get out.

"I've got this. It's not a date, date." Grace laughed and opened the door, sliding out of the car, her nerves rattled.

Ryan met her at the sidewalk. "You don't listen very well," he said, shaking his head and taking her arm as he led her to the front porch.

"And you're mixed up. Don't forget you're only the boss in the office," she teased. He was making it difficult to remember where they'd drawn the line.

Ryan turned to face her, the two of them awkwardly close. "That's true about being the boss. But for once, I don't think I'm mixed up. After tonight, I know exactly what I want. Call it an awakening, if you will." He leaned in closer.

"I don't understand," Grace said, her breath barely above a whisper.

"Maybe this will help." He pulled her up tightly against his chest and lowered his head, claiming her mouth in a toe-curling kiss.

Grace gave in to the inevitable, wanting it as much as he obviously did. She wrapped her arms around his neck, letting him deepen the kiss. Seconds later, he raised his head and looked down at her, his eyes full of tenderness.

"What happened to our business date?" Grace had to ask, needing to hear the words from Ryan.

"I don't know. Somewhere during dessert, I decided this was more like a date, date. I like the idea of kiss and tell better, don't you?" The dimples on his cheeks deepened as he smiled.

Each word he said caused her heart to race faster. If Ryan was to be believed, he cared for her. More than the obvious attraction. It made her breathless to think there might be a chance for something between them. That is until she remembered why it would never work. She stepped back, putting space between them for her peace of mind. "You decided? Since when do you get to decide?" Grace teased, hoping to gloss over their moment of insanity.

If she was able to change Ryan's mind about relationships, what happened when he changed his mind about having kids? Grace had already seen him in action with Holly, and he was a natural. Grace couldn't bear to see the look of disappointment on Ryan's face if they were to become a couple, and then he found out she couldn't have children.

"I don't. We do. You can't tell me you don't feel this connection between us. Whatever it is, it feels real. Something I've never felt before. It's not like I'm looking to get married. I just want to spend time with you and see where this may lead. Or maybe I see renewed hope because of this situation with Bella. I don't know." Ryan reached out and brushed her hair off her shoulder, letting his thumb caress her cheek.

"But what about our boss-employee status?" Grace was struggling to keep the wall between them, afraid of what would happen if it completely fell.

"What about it? It's not ideal, but I am the boss. Don't I get to write the rules? I can change policy if that's what you're worried about."

"Maybe. But who comes out the loser if things don't work out between us?" Her job and her inability to have children was the only thing keeping her from throwing herself back into his arms and kissing him like she'd never kissed a man before.

"Point taken." A look of disappointment crossed his face. It was the truth, and he knew it.

Grace would be the loser. The problem was, she didn't want the night to end.

"Let's just agree to take things slow, and not rush into anything one way or the other. Okay?"

"Okay," she said, unable to say the words that would end what was between them before it even started, but equally unable to jump in headfirst.

Ryan kissed her goodnight and walked away, leaving her staring after him, and wishing he'd taken her in his arms again. Anything she'd felt before dinner had now exploded into a full-blown need to spend time getting to know him. All from a kiss.

Actually, two kisses. She was in big trouble.

Chapter Thirteen

♥

RYAN TAPPED THE END of his pen against the desk as he gazed at the report spread out in front of him. His call with the investors was scheduled for this morning, and he wanted to be prepared. He leaned back in his chair, thoughts of Grace popping in to disrupt his concentration.

He'd acted on impulse and kissed her, breaking every rule he had when it came to business. The problem was... it felt right. At least, it had until she reminded him of what could happen if things didn't work out. His track record with relationships wasn't good, and it wasn't fair to Grace. Torn about what to do, he'd taken the easy way out and settled for somewhere in the middle. It would give them both the chance to think things through.

Not just act on a moment of craziness. Grace came with complications he couldn't afford. Complications like the expectation of marriage and children, things he never wanted. Even the thought of a relationship was more complication than he'd been prepared for a week ago. Only Grace's appearance on the scene had made him question his choices.

He thought about spending his days and nights with her, laughing and teasing, cooking meals together, going places, traveling. All things he'd done by himself, but now he could see sharing those things with somebody else. Someone who made his heart beat faster when she came into the room. Someone who, when he held her in his arms like last night, made him want more. Made him want to be the person she turned to if troubles arose, to be there for her.

Ryan just didn't know if he could trust in love. That was a far reach for him. His phone rang, interrupting his thoughts. "Hey, Harvey. Checking in for the conference call?"

"I am," Harvey said. The older man was one of the investors and the designated person to set up the calls. "Ryan, we are ready to begin the meeting. Larry, Carl, and Jordan are already on the call with us," Harvey said, his tone emitting waves of displeasure like a red warning flag that took Ryan off guard.

"Sounds great. I'm sure you've all had a chance to look at the reports by now. I'm pleased with the first week's numbers, and I hope you are, too." Ryan opened the conversation, disregarding the sense something was wrong. Everyone should be on cloud nine.

"We would be if they were accurate," Larry answered.

"Accurate? What do you mean?" Ryan frowned and glanced down at the report he held. He scanned the document, his eyes immediately drifting down to the tallies at the bottom, but he found nothing wrong.

"Hate to tell you this, but the numbers are incorrect," Larry spoke up. "The accurate numbers aren't horrible, but we missed projections. Not exactly celebration-worthy." This wasn't good.

Grace was responsible for the report. Had she made an error? He glanced down the columns, doing a quick mental calculation.

"Our concern is more about keeping the momentum going forward, and we're concerned about erroneous reporting. Now, while we're certain this has nothing to do with you trying to make the reports look better, it does lead us to wonder about the woman you hired to do the books."

"I hired her," Jordan chimed in. "She came with an excellent reputation and a skill set that included marketing, something we can't ignore. I'm sure this is a simple input error, nothing to get overly excited about."

"I'm pleased you didn't jump to the conclusion I would cook the books. Thanks for that much of a concession," Ryan added sarcastically, his anger simmering just below a boil. It was an insult the thought had even crossed their minds. Unfortunately, Grace was their target. "I agree with Jordon, this is probably a one-off occurrence. It was fairly hectic the week of the grand opening." He rose to Grace's defense automatically but knowing what had really gone on in the office made him wince.

"We have a lot of money at stake, and we have a right to cover our bases. We've heard the woman, Grace, I believe is her name, had a baby at the office the entire first week. If the grand opening was that hectic, how is it that she had time to tend to a baby? What kind of a place are you running over there? A daycare? It's no wonder the numbers aren't right. Honestly, we would've thought you'd run things a little more professionally." Carl was the single largest investor, and his point was valid, making it harder to defend.

For Grace's sake, he would try, but he doubted anything he could say would change how the investors felt about the mistakes. "I do run things professionally, and you know that. My history is proof. Grace ran into a situation and had to bring Holly to work with her. It was only the first week, and for the past week, her sister has been watching the baby. So, we can't blame this on her being distracted." In hindsight, Ryan regretted his words. It would have been easier to leave the blame on the baby.

"Then what do we blame it on? If the woman can't do her job, you need to fire her. Find somebody that can do it right," Harvey said, asking the question Ryan knew was utmost in everyone's mind and laying the consequences on the table.

"I still believe Grace can do the job. I'll talk to her and give her a warning. We need to remember we've asked her to take on a couple of positions in the interest of keeping cost low and should probably cut her some slack. She's amazing with her ad creativity and no one can fault her efforts there. I'll investigate the situation and find out what happened and report back to you all with the new numbers. You'll have updated reports by the close of business today."

The group was silent for a few minutes as they mulled over Ryan's proposal. He prayed what he'd said would be enough to convince them to give her another chance. The last thing he wanted to do was fire her.

"Fine, but no more mistakes, or she's out," Carl spoke first. "We're not trying to be jerks, but this is a business. I hope you understand."

Ryan breathed a sigh of relief. "I do." It was the truth. He knew exactly how he would feel if the shoe were on the other foot. He'd be the one demanding satisfaction. Ryan hung up the phone, running his hands through his hair.

The situation between him and Grace had just gotten ten times worse. Twenty-four hours ago, none of this would've been a problem. He would have reprimanded her, written up the warning, and moved on. But the kiss had changed everything because now, it was the last thing he wanted to do. Instead, he wanted to kiss her again.

Last night's kiss might've been the first and last, but perhaps that was for the best. Then no one would get hurt, and no lines would be crossed. At least the rude reality had hit before they'd taken the next step and decided to go out on an official date.

Somewhere in the middle of the night, Grace had come to the conclusion it would be easier to face things head-on and not shy away from the obvious.

He'd kissed her. *And she'd liked it. A lot.*

Where they went from here was the unknown, but she wasn't going to shy away from the possibility. If Ryan wanted to move forward, then she was willing to try. But in the office, it would be business as usual. Grace wasn't letting any possible relationship interfere with her work. It was important for the other employees to have confidence in her abilities. Outside of work, however, was her own time. And with any luck, the two of them would soon be sharing more of his toe-curling kisses.

"Good morning, boss," Grace called out, pausing in Ryan's doorway.

"Good morning. When you get settled in, can we talk?" There was no hint of the smile she'd come to expect, and his tone was less than desirable. Someone had put him in a bad mood, and for once, it couldn't be her, considering she'd just walked through the door.

"Sure thing. I have a favor to ask, though. Can we keep things business-related at work, and *ummm*, any personal stuff outside of the office? I'd like to keep the two separated, if possible. It's important the other employees don't treat me differently because they think I'm with you." She smiled, but it seemed to go unnoticed. Ryan's gaze was glued to the file he held.

"That sounds good to me." He glanced up at her. "But we still need to talk when you get a second." No hint of a smile. Nothing.

"So, this is a business conversation?" She frowned. "Sorry. I feel like an idiot for jumping to conclusions. Is there anything wrong?"

"Get settled in this morning, and then we can talk." With each word, Grace's anxiety level continued to rise. A sickening feeling washed over her, her gut clenching in worry. None of the laughing, teasing Ryan who'd kissed her last night was present this morning, and his attitude toward her could only mean one thing. She was the one in trouble.

"Fine. Give me five minutes," Grace said, anxious to get whatever it was out of the way.

Ryan nodded and then looked back at the file in front of him, dismissing her.

Grace entered her office and dropped off her briefcase. She took a deep breath, grabbed a cup of coffee, and headed back to Ryan's office. "What's up, boss?" she asked, the casual address as much to lighten the atmosphere as it was to calm her nerves.

"Take a seat." He indicated the chair in front of his desk.

Very stiff and formal. Grace didn't like this side of the boss man. Even with everything they'd been through with Holly, she hadn't felt this unsettled facing off with him. "You're making me nervous." The intensity of his gaze left her fidgeting in her seat.

"I got a call from the investors this morning. There's no easy way to say this, but the numbers you reported are wrong, and the company's sales earnings are far less than your totals. In fact, we came in well below projections based on the information I've been able to put together over the past hour." The leather of his chair creaked as he sat back and glared at her.

This was worse than she'd imagined. "That's not possible. I checked and rechecked the report, and the spreadsheet does all the calculations. I just input the sales numbers."

"Well, the investors say the numbers don't add up. And from what I can tell, it looks like Friday's sales are twice as high as what they should be. Is it possible you duplicated the figures when you transferred them?"

"That doesn't seem likely. I pull the numbers straight from the spreadsheet. I mean, I know I rushed to get it done for you on Sunday, and Holly was fussing, but I still don't see how it could have happened." Holly was cutting another tooth and had been irritable all day, the poor darling in pain and in need of comfort and icy teething rings.

"Well, it did. See for yourself." He turned his computer screen around for her to see and shoved the printed report in her direction. Here are Friday's numbers—" he pointed to the screen, "—and here are your Friday numbers on the report itself. Doubled, it would seem."

"I'm so sorry. I don't know what to say. It's an honest mistake, and I'll fix it." She felt awful about the error, mostly because she took pride in her work, but she felt like his reaction was a tad overboard. Maybe because of the kiss. This was the reason she'd thought a relationship would never work.

"It's not that simple." Ryan shook his head, wrapping his hands behind his neck.

"What do you mean?"

"The investors have a lot of money at stake, and they don't suffer incompetence easily."

The word *incompetence* ran all over her—down to the soles of her feet and back up to her brain. This was insane. Grace stood, unable to sit there and take Ryan's cold judgment without fighting back. Boss or no boss. Based on the way the discussion was headed, it would turn out to be no boss. "Incompetence? It is a simple, correctable mistake."

"From the way you see it. They want to make sure that somebody in a position to handle the reports can do the job they're hired to do. When it comes to money, investors don't like to see any inaccuracies. They worry about fraud and losses."

She placed both hands on his desk and leaned forward, glaring back at him. "Are you firing me?"

Ryan shook his head. "No. Nothing like that."

"Oh. Well, that's a relief," Grace said, stepping back.

"I assured them you are quite competent, and it won't happen again. But I also promised the investors I would write you up with a warning and put you on probation. No more mistakes, Grace. Please. I'm on your side, trust me." He shoved a paper toward her, placing a pen on top of it.

"It doesn't sound like it to me. I went out of my way to do this report for you on a Sunday, and this is the thanks I get? A written warning. If that's being on my side, I can't wait to see what happens when you're not." She grabbed the pen and scrawled her name at the bottom on the line marked with an X.

"You didn't have to do it if you weren't up to the task. You could've said no and waited until Monday." *Was he serious?* Her boss, and the man she cared about—*had* cared about—asked her to do a special favor, and, of course, she'd agreed.

"Remind me not to do anything above and beyond the call of duty for you again," she fumed.

"Sorry, but I don't know your limits. Only you know that. If you couldn't do the reports without the total focus they deserved, you should have said no. People get sloppy when they can't focus. I get that you have a daughter and she's important, but it's a matter of prioritizing and not over committing." His condescending tone rankled, pushing her over the top.

"I see." Buried frustrations from the past two weeks surfaced. "In fact, you know what, I'm going to make this easy on you. I quit. That should make your investors, your partner, and you, all happy. Find somebody else. Maybe they'll be perfect, because I'm not. Apparently, that's a character trait reserved for you and your partners." She started toward the door before she lost her nerve.

"Grace, stop. Please." Ryan's commanding voice ripped across the office, halting her in her tracks.

As much as Grace wanted to walk out the door, she couldn't. Having said the words without thinking first, she instantly regretted them. She needed this job, more than she needed to win this battle.

"I'm not accepting your resignation, because that's not what I'm after here. You're good at what you do. It was just a mistake. I get that. I'm over it. The warning is only a formality because it's company policy. Business is business, and all personal feelings need to be put aside when it comes to World Sport." Ryan was giving her a chance to reconsider.

"You're right about putting personal feelings aside. Something perhaps we should both remember going forward." Grace hoped he was getting her message loud and clear.

"So, you'll stay?" The lack of confidence in Ryan's voice wasn't what she'd come to expect.

Grace breathed a sigh of relief—she hadn't lost her job. "Are we done here? I'll go fix my reports and get them on your desk. Stat." That was the closest she'd come to saying she would stay. She had to try and salvage some semblance of her pride.

"Grace, it doesn't have to be this way." Ryan stood, taking a step forward.

"Yes, it does." Grace stormed out of the office and went into her own, slamming the door behind her. Her life was a mess, but it was of her own doing. The worst part was that Ryan was right. She did say yes to too many people, and usually, that meant taking on more than she could handle.

But Grace couldn't regret taking in Holly. This coming weekend was the last weekend she'd have with the baby, and Grace was determined to make the most of it. No matter what anyone else asked her to do, Mother's Day weekend was off-limits.

Grace spent the next hour going over every number to make sure they were correct. It was true, the Friday's sales numbers had been doubled, but she wanted to make sure all the other figures were double-checked, unwilling to give the investors any other reason to find fault with her work. When she finished, she forwarded it to Ryan.

Pulling up the file for the marketing promo she'd been working on, she began finalizing the details. Grace needed to focus on doing the job she was paid for, not her boss. There would be time enough later to sort out her feelings.

A couple of hours later, her stomach rumbled, reminding her it was time for lunch. Grace headed down the hall, determined to eat in the breakroom. It was high time she started getting to know some of the other employees. Not to mention, it would be a great way to avoid Ryan.

She reached for her phone to call Faith, wanting to check in on Holly. It didn't take her long to realize she'd left it in her office and headed back in that direction, desperate to hear a friendly voice. Faith sharing Holly's antics would be just what she needed to make her day brighter.

A quick glance at her phone revealed a missed call, but Grace didn't recognize the number. Tapping on the buttons to bring up her voicemail, she waited to see who it was before she assumed it was a spam call.

"Hey, Grace, this is Karen. I had to borrow one of the guy's phones, mine's not charged. Listen, things are going good out here, but I'm going to wrap it up early and come home Friday. See you then."

Friday. Grace closed her eyes and shook her head. Karen was coming to take Holly away. The end was coming sooner than she'd expected. That only gave her a few more days. And no Mother's Day. It felt as though someone was ripping her heart out of her chest. Her one chance to be a mom on Mother's Day was being taken from her.

She knew she shouldn't complain. Karen was Holly's mother and the fact she was coming home early to spend Mother's Day with her daughter was a good thing. Grace wanted Karen to be more committed to taking care of Holly, even if it broke Grace's heart to have less time with the baby than originally planned.

On top of everything that had happened this morning with Ryan, this was just too much. Where was the right in all this? She'd given everything to help others, and yet she was the one losing everything. Karen was coming back for Holly, her job was in jeopardy, and she'd lost Ryan before they'd even gotten started.

Grace felt sick to her stomach. She didn't need to talk to Faith, what she needed was to hold Holly. Tears slid down her face, the magnitude of Karen's call and Ryan's warning culminating into a deep ache in her heart.

She pulled a pink sticky note from the pad and jotted a quick message to let him know she was leaving for the day. She stopped at Ryan's office, relieved he wasn't there. Grace stuck the note to the face of his computer so he wouldn't miss seeing it.

Enough was enough and she'd reached the end of her limits. She simply didn't care anymore. For once, Grace needed to take care of herself.

Chapter Fourteen

♥

RYAN WAITED UNTIL IT was just before five o'clock to head back to his office, having stayed out in the warehouse all afternoon. He'd hoped his absence would help cool things down with Grace. She was frustrated with the reprimand, but with the investors breathing down his neck, it wasn't like he had a choice. She'd made it clear their personal lives and business were separate issues, and he'd honored her wish, but at some point, they needed to talk about the kiss.

The best thing to do would be to walk away before things went any further, but he wasn't sure that was an option anymore. *At least not for me.* Grace seemed to have other ideas judging by her comment.

He was surprised to see her office door closed, and when he tested it, it was locked. He glanced at his watch. 4:52. Grace had clearly left early, and it sent him into a wave of panic. What if she'd finished her reports and then quit? She'd do something like that just to make a point. Her headstrong ways would definitely have had her considering it.

He went into his office, glancing at his desk. He spotted the report on top, right where he was sure to see it. A hollow feeling in the pit of his stomach formed. He was almost positive now Grace had quit. Why else would she leave early after receiving a written warning the same day?

Ryan sat in his chair and picked up the report. A spot of pink caught his attention. He pulled a sticky note from his computer and frowned.

Sorry. Had to leave early. Issues with Holly.
Grace

Ryan shook his head, frustration radiating from every pore of his body. She hadn't quit. She'd simply left to take care of the baby. Again. They were operating on two different levels when it came to the job and her commitment to the company.

Short of finding somebody to replace her, he didn't know how to make her understand this was important to him and to the investors. Millions of dollars were at stake. Holly was important, too, but where did one draw the line?

Ryan didn't know the answer, and it's not like there was anyone he knew and trusted that he could ask. Most of the people he dealt with would be quick to tell him to fire her, but that was the last thing he wanted to do. She was a single mom trying to juggle home and office, and he applauded her for those efforts. He just wished it didn't have to be to the detriment of World Sport.

He flipped on the computer and spent the better part of an hour going through his emails, deleting the junk, and then answering the most pressing matters first. He opened the account to review the final copy of the flyer going out this week to well over one hundred thousand sporting enthusiasts' countrywide to advertise World Sport Inc. It was a huge expense but a necessary one if they intended to get the word out. The flyer was well-designed. Eye-catching. And exactly why he was willing to gloss over some of the other issues she ran into.

Ryan clicked the X at the top right of the screen to close the program. He started to get up, only to sit back down and stare at the screen. A niggling of doubt struck him. Something didn't seem right. He reopened the file and scanned the content, searching for what bothered him.

And then he saw it.

The dates for the special were wrong. As in last month wrong. The flyers would be trash worthy at best.

Ryan tried to comprehend the magnitude of what he was seeing. This was far worse than adding up numbers incorrectly. He called the print company, hoping for a miracle. If they hadn't started the order yet, he could make the changes and send them a new file. Problem solved. Except his call went to voicemail. The print office closed at six. He'd drive there personally if he thought it would help, but the office they used was in Colorado. Even a chartered company flight wouldn't get him there in time.

He leaned forward, his face in his hands as he rubbed his forehead, trying to ease the tension building. The investors and Jordon would be furious, seventy-five thousand dollars' worth of furious.

The cost for the wrong flyers and postage and the cost for the replacements. They'd want someone's head on the chopping block, and Ryan knew exactly who it would be. *Grace.* And the only way to be proactive to try and mollify them when they found out was for him to fire her.

It wasn't anything he wanted to do...but Grace left him no choice. The only question that remained was whether to wait until she came in tomorrow morning or to stop by her place tonight. *Neither one was ideal.*

Originally, he'd plan to visit her tonight to discuss their relationship and the kiss, but now, that discussion would be tabled. *Permanently.* He'd always known relationships caused problems with work, and this situation with Grace proved his theory. No matter what he felt for her, he needed to end their business and personal relationship.

Everything he had was tied up in World Sport Inc., and unfortunately, Grace's actions could be costly. And if the investors pulled out either because of the errant expenditures or a loss of confidence in his ability to manage his own people, he'd have no choice but to close the company's doors and try to salvage what he could to start over.

Forty-five minutes later, Ryan pulled into Grace's driveway. It had been a tough decision, but given her inability to find childcare, he decided it would make things easier for her all around if he dropped by her house for the conversation he was dreading. He slid out of the car and headed up the path, one foot in front of the other, his pace slower than usual.

Tap. Tap. Tap. Ryan rapped his knuckles against the front door.

Faith answered, Lucky by her side. "Hi, Ryan." She glanced behind her, as if unsure whether to invite him in.

"Hey there. I need to talk to Grace privately if possible."

Faith glanced behind her again before turning back, her brow scrunched in a deep frown. "This isn't a good time."

Ryan had come this far and had no intention of leaving without talking to Grace. "It'll just take a few minutes. I know she's having problems with the baby, but I need to talk to her."

"You know about the baby?" Faith narrowed her eyes, her expression one of shock.

"Yes. Grace left me a note." Something was going on, making him even more determined to see her. Just because they had to end all personal and business contact didn't mean he didn't care about her.

"Well, in that case, I'm sure it'll be fine. Come on in, and I'll go get her." Faith pushed the door open and started to walk away.

"Thanks," he muttered to her back as she disappeared down the hall.

Ryan knelt to pat the dog while he waited. He could hear raised voices coming from the bedroom. It was a long minute before Grace appeared, her eyes puffy and red from crying. The sight broke his heart and made him rethink what he was here to do. She had plenty of trouble already and he cared about her enough not to want to make it worse. *Except, the investors won't care.*

"If you're here because I left early, I said I'm sorry on the note I left. I just couldn't stay in the office anymore. I needed to be here." Grace tackled the situation head-on, the same way she did everything in life. There was no backing down now.

"I understand, I really do." If it was just leaving a few minutes early, he wouldn't have cared. But this was about so much more.

"You do?" She looked up at him, hope in her eyes. *It wouldn't last long.*

"I do, which is what makes this all that much harder. I'm sorry, Grace. I realize this might be coming at a difficult time, but my hands are tied. It's just one thing after another with you, and this time, I can't overlook it." He shook his head, wishing he had better news to deliver. She looked as if she needed cheering up, not a kick in the butt.

"Are you firing me?" she asked, her tone incredulous.

"You left me no choice."

"Because I left early?" Grace asked, her eyes wide with shock.

"No. Because the file for the flyers you sent to the print company had the wrong date. That's a hundred-thousand worthless flyers being printed and mailed, and I couldn't stop them in time. There's a lot of things I can overlook, but that's not one of them. This mistake will cost the company money we can ill afford, especially at the startup. This isn't what I wanted to happen, and you know it." There was nothing he could say to make this right or better.

Grace looked stunned. "Are you sure? I received an upsetting phone call and knew I had to get out of the office, but I swear I checked the flyer over one last time before hitting send." Grace hugged herself tightly and started rocking. "I'm so sorry."

"I hope whatever is wrong, works out for you. If you'd like, I'll collect your things and bring them by in a few days. I thought it would be easier to tell you here, out of the office, considering we have another issue we should discuss."

Grace's chin rose a notch as she took a deep breath and exhaled slowly. "That would be fine."

"On a personal level, is there anything I can do to help? You look—"

"A mess. I know. But, no, there's nothing you can do. Given the circumstances, however, I think it best if you and I forget what happened the other night and stop thinking of what to do about it. Officially. It's better to leave no doubt in our minds."

Ryan had been ready to say the same thing but hearing her say the words out loud was unsettling.

Final. "I agree. I really like you, Grace, but I think we're at different places in our lives. This would have never worked."

"At least we can agree on one thing. Now, if you don't mind, I think we've said what needs to be said, and I need to get back to Holly."

"Call me if you need anything," Ryan said. It was out of his mouth before he could stop it. The idea of severing all connection didn't sit well, even if it was the right thing to do.

"Doubtful. And I appreciate the offer to drop my things by. It'll make it easier for me."

Ryan turned to leave and walked out the front door and down the sidewalk even slower than when he'd arrived. It felt as though a piece of his heart had been ripped out and scattered on the ground like crumbs on a path.

But in this case, those crumbs wouldn't lead him back to Grace.

Chapter Fifteen

♥

AFTER RYAN LEFT, GRACE couldn't have stopped the tears rolling down her face any more than she could have prevented a volcano from erupting. Even Faith steered clear, playing with the baby in the living room. Only Lucky braved the torrent of her tears and offered comfort, curling up alongside her on the bed. Grace was tired of fighting everything that seemed to be working against her in the universe.

What made it worse was knowing Ryan had every right to fire her. Anyone in his position would have done the same thing. She'd messed up and cost the company tons of money. *I failed him.*

Even a good excuse on her part didn't make the situation better. Clearly, the adoption agency knew what they were doing and had been right to reject her application. As a single parent, she wasn't capable of handling everything without something going wrong. In this case, it had been her job. But what if her shortcomings had affected Holly? Grace wasn't fit to be a single mother, and God knew that far better than she did.

"I take good care of you, though, don't I?" She hugged Lucky, needing the connection.

It was over an hour before she resurfaced and went to find her sister. It was time to pick up the pieces of her life and move forward. "Faith, there's no reason for you to stick around. Now that I don't have a job, I won't need a sitter. And with Karen coming Friday, it's a moot point anyway."

Faith shook her head, her gaze steady on Grace. "Are you sure? You seem like you might need me to hang around. Moral support and all." It would seem some good had come of everything; her sister had grown up almost overnight.

"Thanks, but I'll be fine. I'll still pay you through the week. I know you need to get your car fixed, and a deal's a deal. I'll pack up Holly's things and drive you home." Grace only had a few days left with the baby. Maybe it was a selfish thing to do, but she wanted the baby all to herself. At least Holly wouldn't ask questions if the waterspout of tears turned on again, which was bound to happen.

"Okay, If you're sure. I'll be ready to leave in ten minutes," Faith said hesitantly, coming to her feet and heading down the hall to the room she'd stayed in.

It was more like twenty minutes before they were out the door. Which was still record time for Grace. It figures she'd finally started to figure out how to get her and the baby ready to go somewhere with some degree of efficiency just as Holly was about to go home.

Holly gurgled and blew bubbles all the way to Lancaster, keeping the sisters entertained. By unspoken mutual consent, they avoided any conversation that had to do with the elephants in the car, mainly World Sport, Holly, and Ryan.

She dropped Faith off, not bothering to go inside. Her mother would demand answers if she took one look at Grace's face...answers Grace wasn't prepared to give just yet. Faith would fill her in, and then it was only a matter of time before she'd have to face her mother.

On the ride back to the house, images of Ryan flitted through her mind. Fun times. Family moments. Maybe she'd been premature in walking away from the relationship. She was the one who demanded they keep business and personal separate and then she'd gone and lumped them all together. But then, it's not like Ryan said a thing about the kiss, so it didn't matter.

In fact, he'd almost seemed relieved when she'd made it clear they would be nothing personal between them.

For the next two days, Grace spent every minute playing with the baby, taking hundreds of pictures, or reveling in the joys of parenthood, watching every new thing Holly learned. Sounds and pointing had increased Holly's ability to communicate, making the time together even more special. Grace remembered when she was a child and played house with her dolls at the age of seven. All fun, only now, it was with a real baby who ate, drank, wet, cried, and laughed.

Her phone rang Thursday morning, and Grace checked the screen and saw Olivia's name. She immediately hit the button to answer, worried something was wrong. Olivia worked the day shift and wasn't allowed the luxury of phone calls. But she also knew Olivia's sister had blown into town, expecting to be entertained. At least that's the impression Grace had from the last couple of texts her friend had sent.

"Hey there. What's up?" Grace asked, picking Holly up and moving her to the high chair while she was on the phone.

"Aside from my sister driving me insane and work sucking the life out of me? Nothing." Her friend laughed, easing Grace's tension.

"I'm sorry. I wish there was something I could do to help." Apparently, they were both in need of a pick-me-up.

"There is. You can go to the movies with me tonight. Help me escape this madness." It was something they liked to do frequently for girl's night out, but while she was taking care of Holly it wasn't an option.

Any other time, she would have jumped at the idea. The movies were always a good escape, even if they were only temporary fixes. "I can't. I've got Holly and I took Faith home. And well, Karen is due to arrive tomorrow. I want to spend every minute I can with the baby before she leaves."

"I thought she wasn't coming until the middle of next week. What happened?" The concern in Olivia's voice didn't surprise Grace because her friend knew what having Holly around had meant to her.

"I don't know. Karen called from an unknown phone number and left a message about arriving Friday. I've not heard a word since then." Grace let out a deep breath, trying to calm her nerves. Tomorrow was Friday, and she hadn't been able to stop it from coming.

"Typical Karen. Still irresponsible. How are you holding up?" Olivia asked, getting straight to the point.

"Not good. It's been a rough week. But Holly made it better. We've been having a grand time together. I got fired, you know."

"Fired? You're kidding. Those jerks have no idea—"

"It was justified. I messed up. Ryan did what any other boss would have done." Grace filled Olivia in on what transpired, even managing to touch upon the subject of the kiss and the official breakup with Ryan, even though it had been an unofficial relationship.

"Wow. That is bad. But the job should have nothing to do with any personal feelings you have for each other."

"Maybe, maybe not. But I wasn't all that keen on a relationship anyway, and you know why. I've seen Ryan with Holly, and he's got daddy material written all over him. If he ever gets past his own relationship issues, he'll want children, trust me. And knowing I can't have any, it wouldn't be fair to start anything, so I ended it."

"Sounds premature. Business aside, maybe you should tell Ryan the truth and see how he feels. I can tell how much you like him." Olivia knew her all too well, but it didn't change the facts.

"And risk going through the pain of rejection again? I can't do it. Besides, it's not like he put up any resistance to me ending whatever it was that hadn't started between us. Better to stick with men who don't like kids, and Ryan is not one of them." It's what she'd been telling herself ever since she'd watched him drive away. He wasn't worth the risk.

She still hadn't managed to put him out of her mind, but over time, it would happen. She was sure of it.

"We need to talk. Tonight. I can see why you don't want to leave Holly, but it doesn't stop me from needing some girl time with my best friend. Danny offered to watch the twins, and I'm not letting the opportunity to go off duty slip by. And I can avoid my sister. It's like a double-bonus night, whether it's out on the town or at your place. I'll be over at six. A couple of Disney movies and popcorn sounds like a great alternative to spending the night listening to my sister bemoan her silly troubles as a model."

Olivia was in take-charge mode, and Grace was in no condition to argue. In fact, it sounded like a great way to spend the evening. "That bad, huh?" Grace winced, feeling guilty she hadn't been there for Olivia to help her deal with her sister troubles.

"You have no idea. Besides, I'd love to see Holly before Karen takes her away. She's the sweetest baby."

"Tell me about it." Grace smiled, gazing at Holly, who was rubbing her eyes. Naptime was right around the corner.

"You've gotten too attached. I was worried about this when you told me you'd agreed to help your cousin." Olivia had warned her, and the outcome had been inevitable, but not worth fighting.

"Attached is an understatement. I love Holly to the moon and back. It's my own fault. Honestly. After she's gone, I'll deal with the fallout."

"There's nothing wrong with loving a child, but it sounds like you took it too far. Even this Mother's Day affair you pictured was over the top. You're not her mother, and pretending you are, if even for a day, is not good. Remember, I know you. Self-preservation doesn't usually entail taking one's secret inner desires and turning it into a temporary event. You need to be kind to yourself."

"Well, we don't have to worry about that now, since Holly won't be here. Maybe you're right, and it's for the best." Olivia was trying to keep her grounded, and Grace appreciated her friend's efforts. It just didn't make life fair or any easier to accept in the end. Motherless was motherless.

"We both know this is more about you wanting a child than it is about Holly's mom coming home early. You forget how well I know you."

"Maybe." Olivia was probably right.

"Hang in there and I'll see you at six."

Grace hung up the phone, a fresh set of tears rolling down her cheeks. She only had a couple of hours to pull herself together before Olivia got here. Tonight needed to be fun, not a cry session.

Three days. Six interviews. Zero hope. Ryan sat back in his leather chair, massaging the back of his neck. Even with Grace's shortcomings, she was head and shoulders above the rest of the candidates who'd come in to apply for her job.

Ryan shook his head as he thought of the woman who'd just left. He was astounded at how inexperienced some of the applicants had been, considering he'd told the agency he wanted someone with a minimum of two years' experience in ad design.

This last woman had been straight out of college with no practical application of what she'd learned in school. She'd assumed her looks would trump experience, and had managed to giggle, bat her eyelashes, and nod in agreement with everything he'd said. What the woman hadn't known was that Grace was way ahead of her in both looks and originality.

Ryan flipped through his phone and pulled up his photo gallery, thumbing through the pictures of Holly and Grace he hadn't wanted to delete. He came to the one of Grace and him on the chairlift at the resort the day after they'd met. Her fresh smile could warm his heart with just a glance. The truth was, he missed everything about her.

He made his way to her office to collect her personal belongings. He'd promised to drop them off at her house, not to mention, he wanted to see her again. Ryan grabbed a box from the corner and started loading it, not that Grace had accumulated much in the short time she'd worked here. He picked up the photo of her and Holly she had on her desk and placed it in the box.

After collecting her other things, he spotted her sweater hanging in the corner. He lifted the garment to his nose and took a deep breath. Her scent still lingered, reminding him vividly of Grace. He placed it in the box, his gaze landing on the photo.

In a spur of the moment decision, Ryan pulled the photograph back out of the box. Maybe Grace wouldn't miss it. He taped the carton closed, returned to his office, and placed the picture on his desk. He might not be able to have either one of them in his life, but he didn't want to forget them.

It still bothered him to have let her go. The investors had been livid, and it was only his fast action of firing her that had calmed them down and kept them from walking away from World Sport. Inexplicably, the company's sales numbers had been doing good over the last few days. The only thing they could figure for the increase was word-of-mouth referrals from the first-week sales. Ryan had queued up the ads Grace created for next week, hoping to capitalize on the forward momentum.

He missed Grace and wanted her back in his life, but he wasn't sure what to do about it. A light tap on his door caught his attention. "Come in."

The woman's badge identified her as one of the warehouse employees, but it was her nervous expression that caught his attention. She stayed close to the door, one hand on the doorknob.

"I'm sorry to bother you, Mr. Walker. My name is Melanie Landon, and my sitter isn't feeling well and needs to leave. Do you mind if I clock out early?" She picked at a piece of lint on her slacks, but Ryan assumed it was to avoid making eye contact with him.

Which didn't say much for my employee relations.

The orders were coming in fast and furious, and every person on the team counted. But Ryan's new appreciation for what Melanie might be going through had him answering in a different way than he might have previously done. "That's fine. I'm sure the others can pick up the slack." He'd learned a lot in dealing with Grace and would give anything to have her back and to give her the chance to see how much he'd changed.

"Thank you for being so understanding." Melanie looked directly at him, bolder now that he'd agreed. "If you don't mind me saying so, sir, if your company grows the way you hope it will, one of the best things you can do to attract excellent workers is to offer a childcare center. There are tons of women who would be dedicated to working for you if it was an employee benefit. There'd be fewer absences and happier workers who could see their kids on their breaks and at lunch."

He'd heard it all before, but this was the first time he'd heard it after gaining insight into the difficulties single parents faced. It still didn't make it right for World Sport. "I appreciate your input, and I like that you feel free to present ideas. But unfortunately, that's not a common benefit that companies offer. I hear what you're saying, but I'm not sure that it's viable in our situation. There's not really room for a daycare facility in the building. And I'm not sure the added expense while we're just starting out would be something I could ever sell to the investors."

Melanie stood her ground, his words clearly empowering her to speak her mind. "All you would have to do is bring in one of those mobile units like the schools do when they're overcrowded. It's just a thought. I'm sure there are others like me who can't afford to lose hours on the job, but like now, I'm forced to leave."

Ryan nodded. "It's a good idea. I can't promise anything other than to think about it."

"That's a start." Melanie smiled, lifted her hand in farewell, and left.

What if Melanie was right? In the past, Ryan would never have considered it. But he'd already lost Grace because he didn't have a childcare facility, and now Melanie was leaving early. How many others that he employed would be affected by the lack of onsite daycare? Melanie didn't know it, but she'd struck a nerve in her fast pitch. The employee's ability to provide for their families was of utmost importance to Ryan. It was one of the reasons he paid higher than normal wages. His father's inability to provide and the consequences were still deeply etched on his soul, driving many of Ryan's decisions in life.

A mobile unit. Something he hadn't thought of. Although to be truthful, he'd never given any thought to a daycare facility. Period. Ryan shook his head, unable to believe what he was about to do.

Picking up the phone, he made a few calls, trying to get some sense of what it would cost to put the facility on the property. He researched the licensing required and the added expense. After searching the employee files, he was surprised to discover sixty percent of his employees were women, and of that sixty percent, forty percent had children. And of that number, at least twenty percent had one or more children that weren't of school-age yet, and many of them single.

He ran calculations and discovered Melanie was right. And if these numbers held up against the company's growth and future employee base, they could lose a lot of excellent potential employees, women who wanted to work and needed to provide for their families. The reward far outweighed the expense.

It was the perfect solution, and one he'd present to the investors. He was almost positive he could convince them now that he had all the facts.

And then there was Grace and Holly. If she no longer had to worry about daycare, couldn't he hire her back? World Sport needed her. Ryan needed her. He had a lot of phone calls to make, but come Monday, he hoped to announce a new company benefit.

Ryan felt great about the decision. With a light step, he headed for his car and drove back to his place in Hallbrook, where he would work out more of the details. And tomorrow, he'd pay Grace a visit. He was determined to change her mind about him and the company.

Chapter Sixteen

♥

GRACE WOKE WITH A sense of dread, knowing Friday had arrived. She glanced at Holly, who was sound asleep next to her. Lucky lay curled up at the end of the bed. Last night, Holly had fallen asleep in her arms, and Grace had left her there until it was time to turn in, shortly after Olivia left. Knowing it was her last night with Holly, she'd placed the baby on the bed with her, wanting to keep her close and treasure the moments.

She knew the right thing was for Karen to come home, and she was happy for Holly's sake. The baby deserved a loving mother, and Karen's excitement toward coming home to her daughter was a much-needed change.

But it didn't lessen the ache Grace felt. Within days, she'd fallen hopelessly in love with Holly, and after only three weeks, there was no turning back her heart. Grace would make sure going forward that she played a role in Holly's life, and she'd be there to help Karen whenever she reached out. A forever-free babysitter if that's what it took.

She watched Holly sleep, resisting the urge to touch her soft skin. It wouldn't be right to wake her up for Grace's own personal need to hold the baby close. She turned over and eased out of bed, glancing at the clock. It was already after eight, which was remarkable, considering Grace couldn't remember the last time she'd slept in this late. Sheer exhaustion, combined with emotional turmoil, had finally taken its toll. Although, Olivia not leaving until after midnight had probably played a big part in the equation. It had been great to spend the evening with her best friend and Holly, the three of them having loads of fun. Or, more likely, the two grownups having fun with the baby.

Lucky didn't budge. Grace shook her head and chuckled. "Traitor," she mumbled, picking up the monitor and heading for the kitchen. Grace pressed the button to make coffee after she loaded the plastic cup, picking a bold blend for a little extra wake-up. While it brewed, she glanced around the room. Holly's things were everywhere. At some point, she would need to pick them up and start packing. Karen hadn't mentioned when she would be arriving, and no one had answered the phone when Grace called back.

Not knowing made it worse. At any second, Karen could show up to take Holly home.

Grace sat at the kitchen table, staring into her coffee cup, her finger tracing the handle. Praying for the strength not to give in to another round of tears, she clenched the mug. There'd be plenty of time for tears in the quiet after they were gone.

She got up and went to check on the baby, making sure she was still sound asleep. No noise had come through the monitor, but sometimes, Grace liked to check anyway. It brought her a sense of peace and calmness.

A knock at the front door startled Grace. Karen had never been an early bird, and the last thing she'd expected was for her cousin to arrive at this hour of the morning. She cinched her robe tight while clutching the monitor in one hand, stopping first to close the bedroom door. Lucky must have heard the knock, the dog squeezing through the opening before Grace pulled it shut.

"Glad to see your still my protector, Lucky. It's Karen, but it's nice to know you care." Grace patted the dog on the head and pulled the front door open. To her surprise, it wasn't Karen who stood there.

Ryan.

Her heart went into racing mode almost as if on automatic. The box in his hand with her sweater on the top reminded her of why he was here. That should stall her rush of excitement, but the bouquet of flowers he held kept her heart beating double time.

Woof. Woof.

"Shhh, girl. Don't wake the baby," Grace admonished.

"Good morning. I'm sorry if this is a little early, but I've missed you." Ryan held out the flowers for her to take while he juggled the box in one hand. He stood there looking as handsome as ever with a smile on his face. Based on the way they'd left things last time, the flowers and smile didn't make any sense, just the box of her belongings he'd promised to deliver.

"Thanks. But I don't understand." She laid the flowers on the foyer table and turned back to reach for the box. "Thanks for doing this," she said, her voice stiff and unyielding.

"I'll carry it in, you can take care of the flowers." He stepped inside, not bothering to wait for an invitation.

"Why are you giving me flowers? I thought we had an agreement." She picked up the colorful arrangement and led the way to the kitchen. It wasn't like she had a choice with him already in the door and taking charge.

"We did. But now that I've had time to think it over, I don't agree. We need to talk."

He set the box on the table as she moved to the sink, took a vase out of the cupboard, and added water.

"The flowers are for me because you want to be friends?" she asked, trying to understand. It wouldn't do to misread his intentions.

"No, those are for Mother's Day. To the best mom I know, who puts her baby first for everything." His words were a sucker punch to the gut. At the same time, they were mind-boggling sweet, considering who was saying them.

Grace fought back the tears threatening to overflow. Unfortunately, she lost the battle as she placed the bouquet in the vase and spread them out. They were beautiful. Tears flowed freely, her emotions in overdrive at the kind gesture.

Her very first Mother's Day flowers. Except they didn't belong to her.

"I wasn't trying to make you cry." Ryan moved to stand next to her, taking her by the hand and pulling her close.

"I'm sorry. A lot is going on, and there's no way you'd understand. It's sweet of you to bring these. Thank you." Now would be a good time to tell him the truth. The flowers rightfully belonged to Karen, as Grace was only the babysitter.

She stepped back; her jaw clenched in tension as she let out a deep breath.

"What's wrong, Grace? Don't you like the flowers?" Ryan gazed at her; his forehead drawn tight in confusion.

"No. I mean, yes." She nodded, moving to stand behind the table, picking at an imaginary piece of food from the high chair tray. *Space was good.*

Tell him. But how did you tell someone the baby he thought was yours, wasn't yours, and that it was all a big misunderstanding. It was a lie she'd allowed to continue to save the job she'd lost anyway.

"Where's Holly? I take it she's sleeping," Ryan asked, glancing into the living room.

"Yes. I have a monitor to listen for when she wakes up." She pulled the white monitor from her robe pocket and waved it in the air. It was then Grace realized she was standing there in her robe in front of her ex-boss. *And the guy who'd kissed her.* Everything that could go wrong seemed to have a natural way of finding her lately. Grace cinched her robe tighter.

"Good. I need to talk to you about something. I know how things were left between us, but I've had the last few days to think them over, and like I said, I've had a chance to reconsider. Not having you around has helped me put things in perspective."

"Gee, thanks. Not a very flattering thing to say." She brushed away her tears with the sleeve of her robe. She knew he didn't mean it in a bad way, but she couldn't resist the urge to tease. Apparently, her sense of humor was still intact. It was a good sign that things would be okay. *Eventually.* She just had to trust in God.

"Not what I meant, and you know it," he admonished. "I miss you, Grace." Ryan moved closer, until only the table separated them.

"I miss working with you, too. But it changes nothing. I messed up royally, and you had every right to fire me. Your investors are important, and my mistake cost them money and confidence in my abilities. You don't have to feel bad. I'll find another job. Soon."

"I wasn't referring to the office and our working relationship." He grinned.

"Oh. Then you mean..."

"Exactly. But while we're on the subject, have you had any luck finding a job?" Ryan asked, changing the subject, which made no sense at all considering he was the one who started it in the first place.

"No. But I haven't been looking. I was allowing myself the rest of the week to stay at home with

Holly." She could barely breathe. One minute he was talking work, then personal, then work again.

"Your desire to spend time with your daughter has certainly played into the outcome I'm hoping for." Ryan was talking in circles, but his continued use of the word daughter is what kept reverberating in her head.

"And what exactly are you hoping for?" Grace was trying to keep up but failing miserably.

"Lots of things. But let's start with your job. You're the best there is, and the company needs you back."

"But—"

Ryan held up his hand to stop her. "Let me finish. I understand you made a mistake. A couple of them. But under the circumstances, they're understandable. And as an employer, I've come to the realization that it's a disservice to my employees not to offer childcare at the warehouse."

"What?" Grace couldn't believe what she was hearing, but Ryan's easy smile told her it was true.

"An employee pointed out to me the benefits of an on-site childcare facility, and when I stopped long enough to think about it, I realized she was right.

Productivity goes up, absences go down, and based on the employee pool that becomes available, it's a win-win situation. Everything is being put into place as we speak, and I'm hoping that within a week, I'll have a full childcare facility unit on site."

"You're kidding?" Grace shook her head. It would've been the perfect solution weeks ago, but unfortunately, his daycare facility would come too late for her. "What does this have to do with me? It's a fantastic idea, and I'm excited about what this could mean to World Sport. With cutting-edge benefits, it will attract better employees."

"Exactly what I'm thinking. Including you," Ryan said, moving closer and into her personal space.

"I beg your pardon?" Grace wasn't sure where he was going with this, but she was interested. *More than interested.*

"I want you to come back to World Sport. As an employer, if we'd done our job to make it easier for you to do yours, we wouldn't be having this conversation. The mistakes wouldn't have happened. I consider myself as part of the problem, or at least the company."

"Are you sure? What about the investors?" This was too good to be true. She wanted to work with him, despite the obvious issues of working with a boss she had feelings for.

"Leave them to me. I'm pretty sure I can get them to see why hiring you back is the best thing we can do for the company. They've already agreed to my preliminary plan for the daycare facility."

Grace still hated that she'd let Ryan down. What if it happened again? She wouldn't have the baby as an excuse. And what would happen when she told him the truth about Holly? He might not be so interested in her coming back to work for him. "I don't know, Ryan. What happened with the promo? I feel awful for dropping the ball on the ads, but I was hoping the promo would offset it. Then maybe the investors wouldn't hate me so much, and it wouldn't be awkward to return."

"Promo? I don't know anything about a promo." Ryan's forehead drew tight as he tried to figure out what she meant.

"Oh. Then you probably have something else to be upset with me about. Before I was fired, I'd put together a marketing plan I thought would help the company get some name recognition. Something fun. You weren't around much the last few days I was there, so I couldn't really talk to you about it." More wasted money judging by his cluelessness.

"Do I want to know?" He chuckled, which was the last reaction she expected to get.

"Well, truthfully, I think it was a great idea. It was within my budget, so I didn't need your approval for the expense." Justifying it wouldn't make it cost less, but it made her feel better about the decision.

"Spill it, Grace. What did you do?"

"I ordered ski hats with the World Sport Inc. logo on them." She'd had to move fast to put the campaign in place and had simply taken control, positive it was the right thing to do. "I had them distributed to all the major year-round ski resorts and rental facilities. Any order that came in with the promo code got a free hat. And then I put out a contest to go with it. People had to send in a picture wearing the hat or doing some athletic activity at one of the resorts for an opportunity to win $1000 if their picture was picked as the best." Ryan remained quiet the entire time she explained the plan, his silence making her more nervous.

"That's actually a pretty cool idea." He nodded. "You say you put this into place last week?"

Grace let out a sigh of relief. Ryan wasn't upset with the expense or her. "Yes. The day you, umm, fired me. Why?"

"Our numbers were up this week, and we weren't sure why. We decided it was most likely due to residual sales from the first week and word-of-mouth referrals. But now I have to wonder if it's your promo. Do you have it set up in a way we can track it?" Ryan's excitement was contagious, lifting Grace's spirits considerably. At least something appeared to have gone right.

"Absolutely. When the customer uses the promo code, I can isolate those orders and check the percentage of sales and even the total dollar amount spent if we want to know average sales in conjunction with the promo." Grace couldn't take full credit for the idea as it was a common practice to give out freebies. The contest, on the other hand, was a unique twist she'd added.

"That's fantastic," Ryan exclaimed. "I can't believe you did this and didn't tell me."

"I got fired. It wasn't at the top of my list to tell you what I did that morning," she teased. Grace still couldn't believe Ryan was offering her job back. "But I'm glad you like the idea. There's more you should know, however. Do you remember how you told me you'd be putting inventory at a handful of select resort facilities throughout the country for brand recognition?"

"Yes. We haven't been able to decide where to go so far, although we have a few ideas. Why? Where are you going with this?"

Grace grinned, hoping he'd like this part as well as the rest. "Well, I put into place a way to help you make your selection. As part of the contest, I also let it be known to the participating locations that the top three sales facilities would be in the running for a full-scale review by World Sport Inc. for the next location to open a retail site. I thought it would be a great incentive for the facilities to get the word out to customers. It's a huge drawcard for them to have access to the World Sport inventory at no expense to them, only revenue."

"Wow! What an incredible idea. I can't wait to get back to the office to check those numbers. I'm sure it's your promo that's been driving up the sales this past week. You're a genius." Ryan reached out and pulled her into his arms, hugging her tightly.

Woof. Woof. Lucky seemed to approve the move, as did Grace.

"Thanks. Let's just hope you're right." It felt great to be in his arms again, but she needed to keep her feet on the ground. Grace stepped back. "Oh, and there's even a way you can find out now."

"There is?" he asked.

"The website. There's a link for promo photos. That'll let you know whether the people doing the buying are interactive with the website, which in turn, keeps them in close touch with World Sport's entire inventory."

Ryan grinned as he clinked the link on his phone and clicked on the tab. "Check this out," he said, holding up the phone for her to see. He scrolled through photo after photo that had been posted. "This is amazing! All the more reason to have you on our team. Please, say yes to coming back."

"I accept." Grace smiled, pleased she'd been able to do something to recover from her mistake. Returning to work for World Sport was the best solution, at least it would be once she told Ryan the truth about Holly.

"That's the best news I've heard yet this week. Now we have one other issue I need to discuss with you." Ryan's gaze locked with hers, the intensity more tangible.

"What's that?" she asked hesitantly.

"Us. Our relationship. The one we barely started." He took her hand again and drew her near.

Grace resisted, not willing to fall into his arms automatically, but this time, Ryan held tight. "If I'm coming back to work, we probably need to leave that aspect of you and me alone. Neither one of us is good about crossing lines." She had to make him understand it was better this way.

"That's not acceptable to me. I've missed having you at work, but most of all, I've missed having you and Holly around. I want you both in my life during and after work. I want to give us a chance to see what's real. I've never felt this way about anyone, and it's the first time I'm willing to try. Please say you'll give us a chance?" Every word he uttered would have been perfect if they were based on truth. Something Ryan was missing on a couple of accounts.

Grace shook her head. "It's not that simple. I care about you, too, you know that. But there's something I need to tell you."

"What is it? Nothing will change how I feel about you, Grace. I want you both in my life, personally and professionally. We owe it to ourselves to try." Ryan tilted her head up, his thumb caressing her cheek as he gazed into her eyes, willing her to agree.

"Holly isn't my daughter."

Chapter Seventeen

♥

"WHAT DO YOU MEAN?" Ryan asked, Grace's words sinking into his brain and throwing him into total confusion.

"I should have told you this sooner, but the whole situation got out of control. I'm sorry." She wrapped her arms around her midsection, as if unsure of herself. This was a Grace he wasn't used to seeing. "Holly is my cousin's daughter. Not mine. I'm looking after her, but I'm not her mother."

Her explanation explained the who, but not the why. "But—"

She held up her hand to silence him. "Let me explain, and then you can ask questions. The day before I met you, Karen, my cousin, showed up on my doorstep and wanted me to watch her daughter for three weeks. I know I shouldn't have said yes because I was starting a new job. But I was able to line up my sister to watch the baby while I worked, and suddenly there wasn't a reason to say no. I get that it wasn't the smartest decision, but I've cherished the time I had with her, and in the end, I can't regret it. But I do regret not telling the truth."

He walked to the sink and then back, needing space to think this through. It was a lot to take in. "You just said a mouthful and I'm a little slow piecing it together. What was so important to your cousin that she left her daughter for three weeks?"

"She wanted to go to California to tour with her band." Grace winced as she said the words.

"That sounds irresponsible and immature," Ryan grimaced. Grace had already told him the father wasn't in the picture. Holly's mother was all the little girl had and she wasn't putting her daughter first.

"There's more to it than that and it's not so cut and dried. But Karen's story isn't what's important and debating her choices will get us nowhere."

Grace was right. "I can't believe you would say yes under any circumstances. That's a lot to take on."

Her chin rose in defiance. "It's simpler than you realize. I've always wanted a baby, and this was my chance to have one."

Ryan raised an eyebrow, not buying into her explanation. "But then, why lie about it to me?"

Grace shook her head. "I didn't lie. I never once said she was my daughter. I might not have been clear and let you assume she was, but I never said the words."

He frowned. This was so unlike the Grace he thought he knew. There had to be more to it and Ryan was determined to find out the truth. The whole truth. "That's splitting hairs and you know it. Why would you want me to believe Holly was your daughter?"

Hands on her hips, Grace glared back at him, unwilling to back down. "Because it was my first day on the job. I thought you would be more forgiving if you thought I had childcare problems rather than the truth, which was that I willingly took on Holly's care and brought the entire mess down on my shoulders. And then I was going to tell you that night at O'Malley's, but you got that call and had a woman fired for her excessive personal problems."

He remembered the call, but he also remembered explaining it to Grace afterward. The two weren't on the same level. "That employee's situation was totally different."

"I couldn't take the chance of losing my job. I thought if you knew I was just babysitting, you'd fire me on the spot because Holly wasn't my responsibility, and yet, I'd taken her in without regard to my new employment. Which isn't exactly true, because I did have childcare set up before I agreed to Karen's request," Grace rattled on. Her determination to make him see it from her perspective was most impressive. And it was working. She might have missed her calling and should have been an attorney.

"Not that it helped me in the end anyway. Like I said, it was a chance to have a baby in the house, and I couldn't say no. Holly was just... I mean, it just meant a lot to me. And I thought I had it covered."

There was still one piece of the story he didn't understand. "Apparently, you thought wrong, at least at the time. If you want a baby so badly, why don't you just have one? Lots of women have babies on their own. Or just get married and start a family in the more traditional sense."

Grace visibly flinched. "It's not that simple." She looked away, fumbling with the belt of her robe.

"I don't condone lying, but what's done is done. Holly is a sweet baby, and I can understand you wanting her around. Still, for our working relationship to work, I need you to be truthful with me. At *all* times."

Grace looked up at him. "Agreed." The light in her eyes had faded and he wondered at the cause. He'd forgiven her, and yet it hadn't brought back the smile he wanted to see. None of this changed how he felt about Grace.

"Now back to the subject of us." Ryan moved to stand next to her, taking her hand. "You're telling me Holly isn't a part of the package with you. Am I right?" It was the only difference between what he'd asked for and what she could give as far as he could tell.

"That's correct." Grace nodded, looking away.

Ryan didn't understand what was going on. Why it felt like she was pulling away. He reached out to turn her face back toward him, letting his hand cup her face gently. "I care about Holly, but you're what's most important to me. I want to give us a chance. And, yes, I care for Holly more than I ever expected to care for any child. You've shown me that I'm capable of loving children and of wanting a family of my own. And if you and I go the distance, we can have that one day."

Grace started to cry, the tears slipping down her face. He brushed them away as they fell, more confused than ever. They weren't happy tears. She grabbed his hand and pushed it away, stepping back.

"There's more you need to know. First, Karen's picking up Holly sometime today. I got the message on Monday, which is why I fell apart at the office and had to leave early." Grace took a deep breath and exhaled.

"What is it, Grace?" he asked, seeing her bite down on her lower lip as if trying to find the right words. "We need to be truthful with each other if we are to have a fighting chance at making a relationship work between us."

"You're right. It's just that... The thing is, there won't be a family if you and I go the distance, as you call it. That's why I believe it's better to leave things alone, rather than pick up where we left off only to be hurt and disillusioned in the end. I can't have children, Ryan," Grace said, her voice raw with emotion.

Ryan reached out and pulled her into his arms, wrapping her tightly against his chest. Huge sobs shook her body as he held Grace. Her words had come as a shock, but they also explained so many of Grace's actions over the past three weeks. The desperation to watch Holly when all reasonable adults would have declined. The distress at learning Holly was going home earlier than planned. Ryan was finally understanding the issue. But Grace's inability to have children was something they could weather together.

"Grace, whatever's meant to be, will be. We can adopt. Take in foster children. Do anything we want to do. What's most important is if you and I are meant to be together, the rest will fall into place. What you said isn't enough to make me walk away." Ryan realized it was the truth. Sure, he'd only just come to know he'd like a family, but Grace would be his family, and beyond that, it would be up to them to decide as a couple.

Grace stepped back, brushing away her tears with the sleeve of her robe. "You're a good man, Ryan. But it's not fair to you. I've seen you with Holly, and you'll make a great dad. What if you change your mind? I've lived through a couple of breakups for this very reason. Men who say it's okay and then later, it's not." She folded her arms across her chest as if to ward off the ache surrounding her.

"Any child we would have together, no matter how they come into our family, would be loved. And loving you is what will keep me from changing my mind. I just want us to have a chance to explore what's between us. I feel it here," he said, tapping his heart. Ryan had to make her see the truth and to believe. *In him.*

"The adoption agency already turned me down once. I'm not sure I could handle another rejection." Grace shook her head, and he could feel her pulling away from him.

"But you were single then, right?"

"Yes."

"Well, we'd be in it together. Besides, we still haven't officially dated or declared our love, or talked about marriage. Suffice to say, I'm good going forward as long as I have you. Say yes, and let's see where this relationship takes us. Full disclosure though, I'm pretty crazy about you already." He grinned, pulling her back into his arms. He breathed a sigh of relief when she didn't resist.

"I'm pretty crazy about you, too," she said, a new light shining in her eyes.

Ryan leaned down to seal the deal with a kiss just as a few baby sounds came from the monitor.

"Hold that thought, mister." She grinned. "Duty calls." Grace set the monitor on the counter before heading down the hall.

Ryan knelt, petting Lucky. "Looks like we're going to be seeing a lot of each other, girl." Lucky licked his face, catching him off guard. He laughed, wiping his sleeve across his cheek.

"Good morning, sweet angel. Did you have a good night's sleep? Let's get you out of your wet diaper and into something dry." He could hear Grace talking to Holly through the monitor. Holly's attempts to talk in response, warmed his heart. Babies were so darn cute.

"There you go. Nice and dry. Ryan's here, and I'm sure he'll appreciate you not soaking him. I think the poor man has had enough pee and vomit to last a lifetime."

Holly cooed, and minutes later, Grace came back to the kitchen with the baby in her arms.

Spotting Ryan, Holly held out her hands to him and his heart swelled with love. "Hey, sweetheart. I've missed you." He took the baby from Grace, holding her close.

A knock at the door interrupted the reunion. Grace paled.

Ryan handed her Holly. "I'll get the door," he said, giving her the extra time she needed to compose herself.

Grace nodded silently.

"Hi there. You must be Karen. I'm Ryan Walker. Come on in." The woman's pink and green hair, tight leather pants, exposed midriff, and high-heeled spikes took him by surprise as he held out his hand to welcome her.

"Hi. I didn't know Grace was seeing anyone. And such a hot one at that. Where's she been hiding you?" The young woman laughed, shaking hands with him.

Unsure how to answer the question, he chose not to. "Grace and Holly are in the kitchen."

Karen shrugged and then followed him. "Hey, Grace."

"It's nice to see you again, Karen. I'm glad things went well for you on the tour, but I bet you're glad to be back." Grace was struggling, but there was nothing Ryan could do to help her through this. Except be there when Karen left with Holly.

"The band rocked the tour." The young woman's eyes were lit with excitement as she stepped forward and reached for her daughter. "How's my little girl?"

Holly pulled back, burying her face into Grace's shoulder.

"I'm sorry." Grace looked uncomfortable. "She's grown attached. It's okay, Holly. Mommy's home. Wouldn't you like to give her a hug?"

Holly snuck a peek at her mother and then looked back at Grace, flinging her arms around Grace's neck and holding even tighter if it were possible.

Karen shrugged as if it were no big deal. "Don't worry about it. After three weeks, I'm probably like a stranger to her. Give her a few minutes." It was an odd reaction for a mother to have, not that he knew much about women and children, but something seemed off. "We need to talk," Karen added, glancing first at Grace and then at him.

"You've met Ryan. He's my...my boyfriend, and it's okay. Whatever you have to say can be said in front of him. If it's okay with you, that is." Grace glanced at Karen for confirmation.

Boyfriend. She was accepting his offer. His world was suddenly sunny and bright now that he knew Grace was going to give him a second chance.

"It's about Holly," Karen said, her voice filled with determination. But it was the way she looked at the baby that caught his full attention. Pain. Love. And something else. But he couldn't quite put his finger on the missing piece.

Chapter Eighteen

THE LUMP IN GRACE'S throat made it hard to swallow. Seeing Karen's excitement when she came into the room was a mixture of both joy and sorrow. It was fantastic that she was excited to see Holly. Grace wanted nothing more for the baby, than to have a mother who loved her.

When Holly clung to Grace, there'd been a single second of satisfaction. One she knew was wrong, but not one she'd been able to control. She'd spent so much time with Holly the last three weeks, it was only natural there would be a bond between them—and it was clearly a bond that went in both directions.

Holly trusted her and had come to rely on her. Grace wasn't sure what type of relationship Karen had with her daughter before she'd left, but her cousin's own words indicated a resentment of motherhood. It was a shame, and Grace hoped that time and distance had changed Karen's perspective and that she would now choose to embrace the love and joy Holly could bring her.

"Can I get you both a cup of coffee?" Grace asked as Karen sat at the table.

Lucky sat close by, glancing from one person to the next.

It seemed Ryan preferred to stand, his tall form leaning casually against the counter. "That sounds great. Thank you."

"Yes, please," Karen murmured, her eyes never leaving Holly.

"Here, let me take the baby while you get the coffee." Ryan reached for her, and the little girl smiled and immediately went into his arms.

Grace winced, shooting a look of apology at Karen. She poured the coffee and handed the cups out before taking Holly from Ryan. A second attempt to get the baby to go to Karen equally failed. "I'm sorry. Let's give her more time."

"Don't worry about it. Honestly, it makes this conversation easier." Karen nodded her head as if things were better, not worse.

"What's going on?" Grace couldn't keep the curiosity out of her voice after the odd comment. She sat down across the table from Karen, handing Holly the bottle of milk she'd fixed for her.

"Let me start by saying that what I'm about to tell you has been well-thought-out. It's not a spur-of-the-moment decision. I know there'll be a ton of advice you're going to want to hand out, but please understand I'm nineteen years old. I'm old enough to make my own decisions and to understand the consequences of them. This hasn't been an easy choice for me, but I've decided, and it's final. What I'm hoping is that the decision can be turned into something joyous and wonderful, instead of something sad." Karen was more serious and focused than Grace could ever remember seeing her.

"What are you talking about? You're making me nervous." Grace picked up the bottle from the floor when Holly dropped it. "Here, sweet thing." She smiled at the baby, pushing past the confusion Karen's words caused.

"I'm giving Holly up for adoption."

Adoption.

No! Grace screamed the word inside her head, but she bit her tongue, forcing herself to listen to what Karen had to say, involuntarily clutching the baby a little tighter.

"I've thought about it long and hard, and Holly deserves a mom who can be there for her. Someone who can give her lots of time and attention. I'm not that person. I'm not ready to be a mother, and I can't give her the things she needs. I want Holly to have better than what I can offer."

"You can give her love and family. You would be ready if you quit the band and settled down. Karen, you can't give the baby up for adoption." Grace's heart was breaking for Holly. And for herself, if she was honest. Her one consolation in Holly leaving had been that she would be able to stay in Holly's life in some capacity. If she were adopted out, that wouldn't be an option.

"I'm hoping I don't have to give her up entirely. You're wrong about me. I'm not ready to be a parent, especially not a single parent. But I know someone who is, and I know your fertility issues.

I overheard my mom talking with Aunt Judith. Its why I brought Holly to you in the first place." Karen glanced at Ryan, wincing as she realized what she'd said. "Sorry, I hope that wasn't out of line."

"It's fine." Grace shrugged. Ryan already knew, although he'd only had minutes to come to terms with the information. "But what did you mean when you said that's why you brought Holly to me?"

Karen smiled. "I want you to adopt her. That is if you're up to it. I can see how close the two of you have grown, and it makes this decision that much easier. I hate the idea of giving her up to strangers, but a good home is better than what I can do. With you, Holly and I get the best of both worlds."

Her cousin couldn't have surprised her more. A tiny ray of hope shot uncontrollably through Grace, her dream of having a child being handed to her. But then she remembered the adoption agency's rejection. She knew they'd never approve her to adopt Holly. "I've been through the home study that's required for adoption not long ago, and they rejected my application because of my single status. What makes you think a judge would approve this?"

"Because it would be a kinship adoption. One where all the parties agree and its between family. The hearing is more of a formality than anything else, according to my attorney."

Joy filled her heart, but it came with a sense of guilt. "You're serious, aren't you?" she asked, trying to temper any joy she felt at the idea of Holly becoming her daughter.

"I am." Karen nodded.

Grace glanced at Ryan, who'd stayed silent the entire conversation. She wanted him to jump in with some common sense because hers had fled the scene.

"You realize you're playing with hearts, don't you? This isn't a game. Grace's been through a lot with Holly these past weeks. Her love is unconditional. I can't think of a better person to be Holly's mom, but you, young lady, need to be sure." Ryan's tone had turned fatherly. Direct and straight to the point, Grace realized he was determined to protect her.

Something else to love him for. Grace's gaze drifted to the flowers he'd brought. *Mother's Day.* Once upon a time, she'd been planning a Mother's

Day celebration as a temporary mom, and now, two days before Mother's Day, Karen was offering her the opportunity to make it real. It was like a dream come true.

Karen took her purse from the back of the chair and laid it on the table. "I've made up my mind. And just to prove to you how serious I am, maybe you should look at this." She pulled an envelope from her purse, took out the pages folded inside, and slid them across the table. "I actually got back into town yesterday, but I stopped by the attorney's office to sign some documents."

Grace glanced down at the papers but didn't pick them up. "I love Holly. And more than anything, I want her to have a happy home and to be surrounded by love and family as she grows up. I still believe you can be that person for her, Karen. It doesn't seem right for me to claim Holly as my own. After three weeks, she's wrapped me around her little finger, I can't imagine the pain of losing her if you change your mind down the road."

"I've talked with Mom, and she likes my decision. She said it's probably the most responsible one I've ever made. But then, both of us are hoping you'll adopt her. It's the perfect situation for you. That's the document you need to sign to move the adoption forward to make it legal. The rest of the papers have already been signed and notarized, and you have copies included for your inspection validating what I'm telling you."

Grace's hand shook as she reached out and pulled the document closer for inspection. Just as Karen had said, the letterhead was from an attorney's office.

Petition for Adoption

The words caught and held her attention. For the first time, Grace realized this was real and happening right here in her kitchen. She was finally going to have a child of her own to love and nurture forever, with the bonus it was Holly. A child she already loved with all her heart. Tears welled up in her eyes and overflowed uncontrollably.

"As you can see, I had him draw up the document in your name. It's my greatest wish for you to adopt her. Permanently. As for me, I want to be Aunt Karen, if that's okay with you. This is the best way to give Holly everything she deserves, and for me to at least have her in my life. That way, I won't ever regret my decision. And I'll leave it up to you to decide if you ever want to tell her the truth." Karen's eyes had misted over as she gazed at her daughter lovingly.

Grace didn't know what to think. She held Holly tight, kissing the top of her head. Grace inhaled the fresh baby scent, trying to clear her head. There was no question about whether she wanted to adopt Holly, only the qualms about Karen realizing it was all a big mistake one day.

"What happens if I don't agree?" Grace knew it wasn't a possibility, but she needed to know what Karen was thinking for her own peace of mind.

"I'll still go through with giving her up for adoption, but I'm hoping you'll say yes. My mom's not able to become a mother all over again. Please, say yes, Grace. For all of us," Karen pleaded.

Grace let out a deep breath of air and glanced at Ryan. "Yes. Yes, I'll adopt Holly." *I'm going to be a mom. A real mom.* She brushed away the tears trickling down her face.

Ryan smiled and nodded, letting her know he thought it was a wonderful decision.

Karen jumped up to come around the table and hug her, kissing Holly on the top of her head. "Sweet baby girl, I'm doing this for you. And you've got yourself an amazing mommy now." Her cousin looked over the top of Holly's head, her eyes shimmering with tears. "Thank you, Grace. I'll never make you regret it. I promise."

Ryan moved closer to the table and pulled one of the flowers from the vase, handing it to Grace. "To the newest and best mother ever." He leaned down and pressed a kiss against her lips. "Congratulations, you're going to be a mom."

"I am, aren't I?" A fresh wave of tears rolled down her face, but this time, she let them flow. Tears of joy were the best kind ever.

Karen moved away, letting Ryan stand behind Grace. He kept one hand on her shoulder and one on Holly.

Her cousin picked up her purse. "There's a lot I need to do today, and I'm going to let you enjoy the moment privately. I've got to rejoin the band in three days. If you sign these papers, I can take them back to the attorney's office for him to file. Ryan can witness your signature, which makes this easier.

The attorney will be in contact to let you know what he needs for the hearing and when it will be. But again, the hearing is more of a formality in kinship adoptions since the parties are all in agreement. They like it when children remain with family."

"Karen, are you sure?" Grace had to ask the question utmost on her mind.

"I'm sure. I'll stop by the house and bring you all of Holly's things tomorrow." Karen had become all businesslike, but Grace could tell this was an emotional moment for her as well. Her cousin was a lot more mature and motherly than she gave herself credit for.

Grace picked up the pen her cousin slid in her direction and signed at the X on the line where Karen indicated.

Ryan picked up the pen and signed, witnessing her signature. He folded the papers and slid them back across the table to Karen.

Her cousin slid them back into the envelope and returned them to her purse. "I've got to run." Karen came back around the table and leaned forward to kiss Holly goodbye. This time, her cousin couldn't stop the tears. Proof her heart was in the right place. She was doing this for Holly, and not for herself. Karen left quickly, leaving Grace alone with her daughter and Ryan.

"Didn't see that one coming," Ryan said, grinning down at her.

"Neither did I. This changes everything for me." Grace was still in shock. Holly wasn't leaving, and she was officially the baby's mother. Or she would be once the documents were filed and recorded.

"Hopefully not everything. It's a blessing, for sure. I just don't want it to change anything between you and me. Remember, I told you before you became a mother that I wanted to be with you. Holly's a bonus."

"And a beautiful bonus at that," she said, smiling down at her new daughter, love vibrating from every pore of her body.

Chapter Nineteen

♥

RYAN SWUNG THE DIAPER bag over his shoulder and turned to watch as Grace pulled on Holly's sweater. Lucky lay on the floor, not far away, her tail thumping the ground occasionally as her eyes darted toward the door. She'd be disappointed not to be included in today's action, but it's not like they could take the dog to church.

He leaned down to scratch Lucky behind her ears. "Sorry, but you can't come with us, girl. I'll take you out as soon as we return." Ryan chuckled when the dog licked his hand.

Today was a special day, and Ryan was eager for it to unfold, having several surprises for Grace. Ryan knew what was in his heart without any lingering doubts. All he needed was the right moment to tell her, and he prayed she felt the same way.

He couldn't wait to share the news that he'd received an email from Bella and that his sister wanted to meet him. If it wasn't for Grace's insistence and urging, he might have never had this chance at a reunion with his long-lost sister.

Bella's email told a different story than the one he'd let himself believe. Ryan read the regret in her words and sensed her sincerity in the request to meet in person. After much deliberation, Ryan had emailed his sister back and agreed.

She was coming to Hallbrook. After letting down the final guard around his heart, he was ready to move forward and see what the future would hold.

"Ready to go?" he asked, smiling at the beautiful pair of ladies in his life.

"Absolutely." Grace's lovely smile was all the reward he needed for the extra effort he'd gone to get a table at O'Malley's for their special Mother's Day brunch. Everyone knew and loved Grace, and her new bundle of joy was cause for celebration.

"Just so you know, I did call Karen to invite her today, but she declined. She didn't want to take away from your moment." Ryan hadn't been sure what to do but had gone with what felt right. In the end, it worked out the way he preferred, but he'd been willing to go the extra mile for Karen. After all, she was the one who'd given Grace her greatest dream.

"She could have come. I wouldn't have minded."

"I know you wouldn't. You have a huge heart. It's one of the things I love most about you."

"You do, huh? I like the sound of that." Grace smiled over the baby's head at him.

Ryan stopped, empowered by the love shining in her eyes. "Grace, I know I haven't always made things easy for you, but it doesn't change the outcome of the time we've spent together. I love you with all my heart, and I want to be with you. Always."

Her eyes grew wide, filling with tears. Happy tears judging by her expression. "I love you, too. I have for a long time, even if I tried to talk myself out of it." She stepped into his embrace.

Everything dear to him was in his arms, as he dropped a kiss on the baby's cheek before lowering his mouth to Grace's, pouring every ounce of his love into the kiss.

Holly pressed a finger into his cheek, and then his eye, forcing them apart.

"Hey, you," Ryan said, grabbing her finger. "I know it's time to go. Thanks for the reminder."

Grace laughed. "Give me a second to run down my mental checklist. I'm only just getting the hang of this parenting thing."

"It won't take you long. You can do anything you set your heart on." Ryan pulled open the door and waited.

Grace's smile faltered slightly. "I feel bad Karen's not ready to be a mom, but I'm thrilled beyond words to have Holly as my daughter. It's a mixed bag of emotions for sure, but in the end, I have only to focus on Holly and trust in God that this was the plan. I'm going to find a bigger place to live, and since I got my job back, I can afford it."

"Your boss is a softie from what I hear. You should hit him up for a raise." He winked. They'd agreed that come Monday morning, Grace would return to work with Holly. It wouldn't be long until the childcare facility was up and running and the licenses procured, and until then, he would help her take care of the baby. They would be a team in and out of the office.

"A softie? *Hmmm*...jury's still out on that one. I'll wait till my annual review for a raise like everyone else, but be prepared, I'll come loaded with stats to back up my increase." She flashed him another of her golden smiles as he took the baby and strapped her in the car seat.

"I have no doubt of that." He shook his head and chuckled.

Ryan drove to church and pulled into the parking lot. The parents-with-babies spots were filling up fast, Ryan parking in one of the last ones available.

"This is exciting. I've never been able to park this close." Grace smiled as she slung the diaper bag over her shoulder and pushed open the door.

Ryan slid out of the car and opened the back door, intent on getting Holly. "One of the many benefits of having a baby. Get used to them." They walked inside, hand in hand, and went in search of the nursery.

"I'd like to register my daughter if I could," Grace told the young woman monitoring the entry.

"Sure thing. If you step inside, Anna will take care of that for you." She pointed at a young woman who stood off to the side of the room in front of a podium with a laptop computer.

It didn't take long to give the woman the information, and in return, Grace now had a vibrating beeper in case they needed her for anything. Ryan liked the smooth efficiency and the care given to protecting the children. It had been a long time since he'd been to church, but it felt right for several reasons today. God had brought Grace, Holly, and Bella into his life, and Ryan had much to be thankful for.

Pastor Richard's sermon touched on love and family and hope, the message strong and powerful. Ryan let every word push him toward a better understanding and acceptance of the situation with Bella.

"That was a beautiful sermon. I hope Holly did okay," Grace said, holding Ryan's hand.

She started to rise, but Ryan resisted, encouraging her to sit back down. "I'm sure she's fine. You haven't vibrated at all this morning." He laughed. "I want to share something with you."

"What is it?" Grace asked, sitting down beside him.

"I heard from Bella last night and she wants to meet me. And I've agreed."

Grace grinned, her eyes lighting up in excitement. "You did? That's great. What did she have to say? Tell me everything." Women liked to be right and Grace was no exception.

"The short version is that after she was placed with a new family, they moved away. Apparently, she called the agency several times to talk with me, but they wouldn't give out personal information regarding my placement. After she turned eighteen, Bella started writing letters to the agency a couple of times a year, hoping to find out where I was living. The agency claimed they talked to my foster parents to see if they were agreeable to a meeting, but they always said no.

"And after I turned eighteen and aged out of the system, the agency lost track of me for a while. Bella never stopped trying to find me. It was only like five years ago when I contacted them regarding some personal information I needed, that they got a new address for me and started sending me letters every so often, indicating Bella's request for my information. Unfortunately, I wasn't in agreement for my own misguided reasons and always said no. Until you changed my mind."

Grace hugged him, her joy overflowing. "I'm so happy for you."

"Last night, I emailed her back and agreed to meet but I still had some mixed feelings about my decision. But after today's sermon, I know this is right. I'm looking forward to when Bella arrives."

"I think that's the best decision ever. I'm so proud of you. Tell me what you know about her. This is fantastic." Grace excitement was contagious, not that he didn't already have some of his own brewing.

"Bella's a nurse and lives in California, is married, and has three kids. I'm an uncle, if you can believe it? Three times over." Ryan grinned. He couldn't wait to meet his niece and nephews, but unfortunately, it wouldn't be this trip. Bella wanted the two of them to have a chance to get to know one another again, without the added pressure of tossing kids in the mix.

"That's incredible. You're going to be a wonderful uncle, I'm sure. Remember, I've seen you with Holly. I have it on good authority you're a softie," Grace teased.

"The best decision I ever made was not letting you out of my life." He brought her hand to his lips, his kiss more reverent and meaningful in the house of God. Like a promise.

Grace rewarded him with one of the heart-warming smiles he loved so much. "When's she coming?"

"Next week. Bella was anxious to meet. She thought we'd waited long enough."

Ryan took her hand and they left the sanctuary to pick Holly up from the nursery. They still had to get to O'Malley's for their reservation and his next surprise. The place was packed when they arrived, but the server led them right to their table.

Grace looked up at him, her eyes lit with joy as she spotted her mother and sister already at the table. "You didn't tell me they were coming."

"What can I say? I'm addicted to the smile that comes with surprising you." He leaned over and dropped a kiss on Grace's forehead, doing the same with Holly. *My package deal.*

"Hi, Mom. Faith," Grace said as Ryan pulled out a chair for her at the head of the table, Holly's high chair next to it.

Grace was the guest of honor today, even if her mother was also celebrating. A first Mother's Day was always special.

Faith reached for Holly, happy to see the baby. "How's my little munchkin?"

"She's doing great. And a happy baby makes a happy mom," Grace said, laughing.

Ryan could tell she was bursting with excitement to share the news, something he'd let her do in her own time.

"Speaking of, I thought you said Karen was picking her up Friday?" Judith asked. It was all the opening Grace would need.

"She was, or so I thought. I have news. Big news," Grace said, enjoying the moment of suspense.

"What is it, honey?" Grace's mother asked, reaching over to take Holly from Faith. Everyone wanted a piece of the baby action. Holly would never have a shortage of love all around her as she grew up.

"We have a new member to welcome to the family." Grace's grin reached from ear to ear, the light shining in her eyes full of love as she glanced at her new daughter.

"You're getting married?" Judith asked, a stunned expression on her face.

"You're pregnant? I thought..." her sister said, stopping before she completed the sentence.

They were both on the wrong track, but Ryan couldn't help the tiny twinge of pleasure that came with the thought of him and Grace doing both. Getting married and having a baby. He'd come a long way in his line of thinking since meeting Grace, and at times, it still surprised him.

"It's not what you're thinking. You all know that can't happen." Grace stood, picked up Holly, and turned back to the table to make her big announcement. "But I would like you to meet Holly soon-to-be Baxter, my daughter." Grace beamed, kissing Holly's cheek.

The name change had been agreed upon by Karen as the best way to keep Holly from growing up confused. When the time was right, Grace would tell her the truth about Aunt Karen.

"What? Whatever do you mean?" Judith asked.

"Karen gave Holly up for adoption. To me. I'm her new mom, or I will be once the legal proceedings are finished." Grace said the words as though they were the most cherished words she'd ever uttered.

"What a surprise. I can't believe my sister never said a thing," Judith said, staring up at the baby. "I guess that makes you my new granddaughter, sweet pea." Holly reached down to pick at the hair clip in her grandmother's hair.

"And I'm Aunt Faith. I love it." Faith got up to hug and kiss Holly, overjoyed with the news. "Congratulations, Grace." She hugged her sister.

The women took turns holding Holly, fawning over the new addition to the family. Poor kid must feel like she was on a merry-go-round. Not one to be missed, Ryan equally took his turn to capture his favorite baby's attention.

"By the way, what's Ryan doing here? I thought you lost your job," Faith asked, looking back and forth between the two of them.

Judith's joy cooled considerably. "You lost your job? And you have a new baby. Oh, my."

"She did lose her job. It was a temporary moment of insanity on my part, and I've convinced her to come back to work for me," Ryan spoke up, feeling he was the one that owed them an explanation. It was better to take any blame off Grace. He wanted today to be perfect.

"That still doesn't explain why you're here," Faith pressed the subject.

"I'm here to celebrate Grace's first Mother's Day with her because I care about her and Holly, and not just professionally."

"So, you love her?" Faith asked, charging ahead for the answer she wanted to hear. She'd make a great aunt and protector for Holly, the same way she was doing for Grace.

Ryan laughed and nodded. "I do."

Judith and Faith wore equally stunned faces as the server approached the table, topping off their juice and coffee, and giving the two women a chance to recover.

Ryan's phone rang, breaking the silence. "Sorry. It's Jordan, and I should take this."

"Go right ahead. The food should be here any minute," Grace said, eyeing him with interest.

"Hey, Jordan. What's up?" Ryan asked, lowering his voice out of respect for the others at the table.

"I wanted to let you know I checked into the promo code you sent me, and the sales are no coincidence. The numbers are up because of the marketing plan Grace put into place. You've got to hire her back. And hire someone else to be your assistant. We want her full-time in marketing. Stat."

He'd sent the info to Jordan, hoping to get answers before the weekend was over. Preferring to spend his time with Grace and Holly, he'd entrusted his partner to do the legwork. After all, Jordan was the one who'd hired Grace in the first place, and it was a great opportunity for him to prove he'd made the right decision.

Ryan didn't need the numbers to know she was perfect. "Relax. It's already done." He glanced over at Grace, only to find her watching him, curiosity in her expression.

"What? How did you make that happen?" Jordan grilled him for answers.

"I've got my ways." He chuckled. "But I'll tell her the good news. I'm with her now at O'Malley's."

"Interesting," Jordan said, his tone more questioning than stating a fact.

"Yes, very," Ryan agreed, laughing as he disconnected the call. He took Grace's hand, a move both mother and sister didn't seem to miss as all eyes turned to him. "Jordan just confirmed that our success last week was due to you and your remarkable idea, and he said to hire you back. Stat." He chuckled. "Told you I could handle the investors. He also said not to let you get away. I think he's right." Ryan lifted her hand to his lips. There would be no doubts left at the table as to his affection or intent.

Grace blushed. "Let's just hope you don't change your mind the next time I make a mistake," she teased.

"The mistake was all mine in letting you go. A man likes to think he's learned from his mistakes. I don't intend to let it happen again, personally or professionally."

Holly started bouncing up and down on Grace's lap, demanding her full attention.

"Mama," Holly said, much to the excitement of everyone at the table.

"Did you hear that?" Grace said, her eyes tearing. "She said it once before, but we weren't sure, and I wasn't her mom, but I am now." Grace hugged the baby. "Yes, honey, I'm your mama. Say it again. Ma-ma." Grace was using her baby talk voice, something she did frequently.

Holly grabbed for Grace's earring, ignoring her mother's attempts for a repeat performance.

Sitting around the table amidst laughter and fun, Ryan realized what he'd been missing in his life. *Grace had turned out to be his saving grace.* Ryan leaned over to whisper in Grace's ear. "I love you. Today, tomorrow, and always. Both of you."

Grace flushed with pleasure, her gaze full of love. She didn't have to say the words, he could feel the emotion radiating from her.

"I love you, too." She might not have had to say the words, but he sure liked hearing them.

He leaned in, intent on kissing her, but Holly had other ideas. She reached out, wrapping her arms around their necks, pulling them together for a group hug.

Epilogue

S IX MONTHS LATER...

Grace watched as Holly ran toward Ryan, her arms outstretched. "Daddy, Daddy, pick up," she asked. It was one of Holly's favorite games when Ryan would lift her over his head and play helicopter. Lucky ran around the yard, barking excitedly and joining in the game.

Married now for five months, Grace's love for her new husband and daughter continued to grow. Ryan was leaving the option of adopting another baby up to her, a decision she'd put off making until things settled after moving into their new home. The house had a huge backyard much to the delight of Holly who loved swinging on the swing set, and to Lucky who simply loved being outside.

During that time, World Sport Inc. had grown at a rapid pace, and two new stores had been set up based on the results of her marketing contest. Grace had been more than relieved when Ryan opted to let Jordan open the new locations, choosing instead to stick around New Hampshire with her and Holly.

Bella's visit had been a blessing. Time and conversation managed to put the two siblings back on the same page, and Ryan had even flown to California to meet his niece, nephews, and Bella's husband, Glen. And now, they all were coming for Thanksgiving. Luckily, the new house had plenty of room.

The only problem was that between Holly, maintaining a full-time job, and then buying a new house and moving in, Grace had worn herself out to the point of exhaustion. With Bella coming next week, she'd finally relented to Ryan's suggestion that she make an appointment with Dr. Duncan.

Ryan was a worrywart for sure, even staying home this morning to take her to the Hallbrook Medical Center for her appointment. The place was five minutes down the road, and yet he insisted on driving.

Grace hadn't let on, but she was secretly relieved he was with her. This morning, she'd felt worse than usual, not to mention, her stomach was bloated, and she'd been gaining weight. It was as though her polycystic disease had returned. Her symptoms resembled everything she remembered from when she'd been diagnosed at the age of eighteen.

She'd been telling everyone she was just tired and under the weather. Now, she wasn't so sure. Maybe her hormone prescription wasn't strong enough anymore and needed to be adjusted.

"Ready to go," Ryan asked, walking past her with Holly on his shoulders, but not before he leaned over to kiss Grace.

"Of course. Let me get my handbag." Grace had explained her condition to Ryan but hadn't told him she thought it was flaring up, not wanting to worry the worrywart.

He buckled Holly into her car seat and then drove them to the medical center.

"If you get Holly, I'll go get checked in," Grace said, grabbing the diaper bag and her handbag.

"Gotcha." He smiled, his gaze lingering on her, love in his eyes.

Grace never grew tired of that look. It was reserved for her and only her, making her feel like the most cherished woman in the world. She checked in and then joined Ryan where he'd taken a seat in the lobby. They didn't have to wait long before Grace was called to the back. Of course, Ryan came with her.

"Good morning, Dr. Duncan. Thanks for seeing me on such short notice." Grace smiled, and the two men shook hands.

Ryan moved to sit down on the extra chair, trying to keep Holly occupied.

"Good morning. And no problem. I always like to leave a few slots open for established patients with unplanned needs. So, what seems to be going on?" Jake had become the town's doctor when the old doctor retired several years ago. Other than annual physicals to keep her hormone prescription filled, Grace avoided doctor's offices, having had enough of them when she was younger.

"I haven't been feeling well the past few months, but I brushed it off as exhaustion from all the recent family and life changes." She shot Ryan a smile, knowing all the changes were happy ones involving him.

"I see. Any nausea, headaches, or vomiting?" Dr. Duncan asked.

"Some nausea for sure. No to the others. I'm bloated and putting on weight, but that could be because I'm eating more regularly now that I'm feeding a family."

Dr. Duncan smiled. "Have a seat on the table and let me check a few things out."

Grace did as he told her, hoping for a quick answer and the solution.

"How have you been sleeping?" he asked while using the stethoscope to listen to her heart.

"Not well. I toss and turn a lot." At one point, she'd blamed it on the extra body heat in bed from her husband, but even a fan hadn't made a difference.

"Take a couple of deep breaths," he instructed.

Grace inhaled and exhaled several times as the doctor moved the stethoscope around to listen to her heart and chest.

"Everything sounds good. Any change in your periods?" he asked while using a light to check her eyes, ears, and nose.

"No. Irregular as always from the polycystic ovary syndrome. If anything, they are shorter." Grace shrugged. "I was wondering if my hormone dose might not be strong enough anymore."

"It's possible. But we have a few other things I'd like to check on before jumping to that conclusion." His smile reassured her he didn't think anything major might be wrong. "I'd like you to give a urine and blood sample while you're here. The nurse will coordinate it, and then I'll be back in, and we can talk some more."

"Sounds good."

Dr. Duncan walked out after stopping to talk to Holly, making her giggle when he blew up a latex glove and handed it to her.

"So far, he doesn't sound overly concerned, which is a good sign," Grace said, hopping off the table. She hated having her blood drawn, but in order to find out what was going on, it wasn't like she had any choice.

"I agree." Ryan smiled, setting Holly down. "I'll wait here for you. The last thing I need to see is you getting blood drawn."

"What? The mighty Ryan is a coward when it comes to blood?" She grinned, loving him even more for being willing to admit a weakness, especially since it was a weakness they shared.

"Yup." He laughed, burying kisses into Holly's neck and trying to make her laugh with him.

Grace left the room to talk to the nurse and the lab tech, wanting to finish up and go home. A nap sounded heavenly right about now, especially since she'd taken the whole day off for a change. Ten minutes later, she was back in the room with Ryan, waiting on the test results.

"Mama," her daughter said, holding out her arms.

Grace took Holly by the hand and walked her around the room, pointing out pictures to keep her distracted and happy while they waited. They took turns as the entertainment committee, a toddler easily bored in a doctor's office. Twenty minutes passed before Dr. Duncan returned, his nurse right behind him and pushing a machine into the room.

Grace looked at Ryan for reassurance, fear settling in.

"What's going on? What did you find out?" Ryan asked, the concern in his voice matching her own.

"Quite a bit, actually. Nothing for you to worry about, honestly, but I'd rather show you than tell you. Grace, if you'll lie down on the table and lift your shirt, I'd like the nurse to run an ultrasound on your belly."

It couldn't be bad, not if they were smiling. And he said not to worry. Grace took a deep breath and lay back. Ryan stood next to her and held her hand, trying to manage Holly at the same time and keep her quiet.

The nurse prepared the machine. "I'm sorry, but this gel is always so cold. I've got to rub it on your belly for us to get a good picture."

"That's fine." Grace took another deep breath, calmed by Ryan's presence.

It wasn't long before the black screen was lit up with gray lines and shapes. The nurse rolled the head of the device around, stopping when she located what she was looking for.

Dr. Duncan moved closer and pointed at the screen. "See this area here?"

"Yes," she said, not sure what she was looking at.

Ryan squeezed her hand reassuringly.

"Turn up the volume, Janet," Dr. Duncan told the nurse.

The nurse smiled, reaching for the button. A low pounding noise came from the machine.

Grace glanced at Dr. Duncan. "What is it? Is something wrong?"

"Not at all." He grinned. "I'm guessing everything is right. Grace and Ryan, I'd like you to meet your son."

Son. That meant she was pregnant. It wasn't possible. She looked at Ryan to see if he'd heard the same thing. His shocked expression was one of pure joy. He *had* heard the same thing.

"But I don't understand. How is that possible?" Grace asked, tears streaming down her face.

"PCOS can be hard to predict. Every woman is different, and, yes, fertility is a huge problem, but not always. Clearly." Dr. Duncan winked, his smile growing wider.

"But how? My periods?" Grace was afraid to believe.

"Aren't regular. PCOS interferes with your body's normal messages when you get pregnant. I'm guessing you won't have anymore, or at least until after the baby is born. You're about four months along judging by the size of the baby."

The flood gates opened on her tears as Grace accepted what the doctor was telling her. God had blessed her and Ryan with a son. Holly was going to have a baby brother.

Ryan kissed her, tears streaming down his face. He brushed them away and looked at the doctor. "You said a son. How can you tell?"

"Janet, zero in on the image and show Ryan how we know."

The nurse laughed and tapped the machine to enlarge the picture.

"There. That's his boy part." The doctor pointed to the screen.

"*Umm*, I must not be seeing what you see," Ryan said, totally confused. "It doesn't look like much."

The doctor and nurse chuckled. "At twenty weeks, that's all your son has—not much."

"A son. Ryan, we're pregnant." Grace couldn't stop crying. She wasn't sick. It wasn't her PCOS. It was a good old-fashioned pregnancy.

Holly reached out toward the machine, trying to join in the fun.

"That's your baby brother, sweetheart," she told her, pulling Holly's hand toward her mouth to kiss it. Once upon a time, Grace hadn't been sure she would ever have a child, and now she had two.

Grace gazed at Ryan, sharing in the joy of the moment. It was a miracle. "I think we should name him Caleb, after your father," she said, hoping he'd agree. Ryan had made peace with Bella, and it was time for him to make peace with his father. People make mistakes and hurt you, but it was forgiveness that set you free.

"That sounds perfect. Just like you are." Ryan held her hand as the nurse took several pictures for keepsakes, and then the doctor and nurse turned to leave.

"Miracles deserve a little extra time, so I'll let you three share this moment with baby Caleb a little longer. Oh, and by the way, in case you haven't figured it out, that pounding is his heartbeat." The door closed behind them.

"I love you, Mrs. Walker," Ryan said, unable to take his eyes off the screen. "This is such an incredible blessing."

"I agree. And I love you, too, Mr. Walker. Holly doesn't understand yet, but she will soon. I think she's going to make an amazing big sister." Grace kissed Holly on the top of her head—and soon, she'd do the same for Caleb.

What to read next?

Love & Liberty
Book 6 of the Holidays in Hallbrook series – A Sweet Independence Day Romance.
Blinded by the past, it takes a little fate and great faith to be liberated and set free. Where you fly is up to you...

If you enjoyed this sweet and charming romance, be sure to check out the ALSO BY ELSIE DAVIS section on the next page for more clean and wholesome romance.

BONUS READ

Want to keep in touch with new releases and what's happening in the world of Elsie Davis?
Sign up for the monthly newsletter at Elsie Davis HEA (Happily-Ever-After) and enjoy DIGGING THE DRIVER (A Celebrity Corgi Romance) as a FREE BOOK!

The greatest compliment you could give an author is to leave a review in order to help other readers discover the same great stories you enjoyed. Amazon/Bookbub/Goodreads are all great places. Many thanks!!!
Another great way to keep in touch - *Follow Elsie Davis on FaceBook*

Also By Elsie Davis

Sweet, Clean and Wholesome Stories...with a Happily-Ever-After Guarantee!

Holidays in Hallbrook
(Sweet Romance Series for Holidays Throughout the Year)
Welcome to Hallbrook, New Hampshire. A small-town filled with the unexpected, lots of love, and of course, a beloved dog to ramp up the excitement.
Love & Order (Labor Day)
Love & Family (Thanksgiving)
Love & Peace (Christmas)
Love & Chocolate (Valentine's Day)
Love & Hope (Mother's Day)
Love & Liberty (Independence Day)
Love & Honor (Veteran's Day)

Love & Joy (Easter)
Love & Adventure (Father's Day)

Great Smoky Mountain Getaways
(Christian Inspirational – Women's Fiction Romances)
Juliet's Journey to Love
Poppy's Path to Love
Rachel's Road to Love

Crossroads Creek Cowboys
(Christian Inspirational Romances)
The Heart of a Cowboy
The Help of a Cowboy
The Return of a Cowboy
Coming Soon – The Care of a Cowboy

Crestfield Inn Romances
If you like special kinds of soulmates, a splash of
the supernatural, and wholesome relationships,

you'll adore this sweet bit of fun filled with romance and mystery.
Turning Back Time
Turning Up Roses
Turning Down Pie

Celebrity Corgi Romance
(Standalone Sweet Romance)
If you like light mystery mixed in with your happily-ever-after, you'll enjoy this second-chance romance and the race to save an adorable Corgi.
Digging the Driver

Gold Coast Retrievers
(Sweet Romance)
Special Golden Retrievers help their humans solve mysteries, save lives, and even find love...
Defending Dakota

Trinity River
(Sweet Western Romance)

Ranchers and farmers depend on the Trinity River for water, but when a secret conglomerate starts buying up property by fair means or foul, it's time for the landowners of Tumble County to fight back—Texas style. But what they don't count on, is finding love in the process.
Back in the Rancher's Arms
Small Town, Big Secrets

Coming Soon! (2023-2024)

Sundancer's Legacy – 9 Book series

Sundancer's Star
Sundancer's Joy
Sundancer's Heart
Sundancer's Majesty
Sundancer's Miracle
Sundancer's Glory
Sundancer's Kiss
Sundancer's Moon
Sundancer's Splendor

About The Author

Elsie Davis is a *USA Today and International Bestselling Author* of over 25 sweet, clean, and wholesome romances, and a member of the ACFW. She discovered the world of Happily-Ever-After romance at the age of twelve when she began avidly reading Barbara Cartland, the Queen of Romance, and has been hooked ever since. After building her dream log home on top of a small mountain, she turned her attention to do what she loves most, writing. Elsie writes sweet Contemporary Romance and Contemporary Christian Romance from her heart...hoping to share a little love in a big world.

When she's not writing, she can be found birding, kayaking, camping, fishing, playing disc golf, and taking nature walks—hoping to spot wildlife. Basically, she loves all things outdoors, EXCEPT cold weather. She and her husband are avid Caribbean cruisers, but Elsie's favorite vacation was their cruise to Alaska. (In spite of the cold!) Indoors, she enjoys a toasty fire, and of course, a great romance with a guaranteed Happily-Ever-After.

https://www.elsiedavishea.com